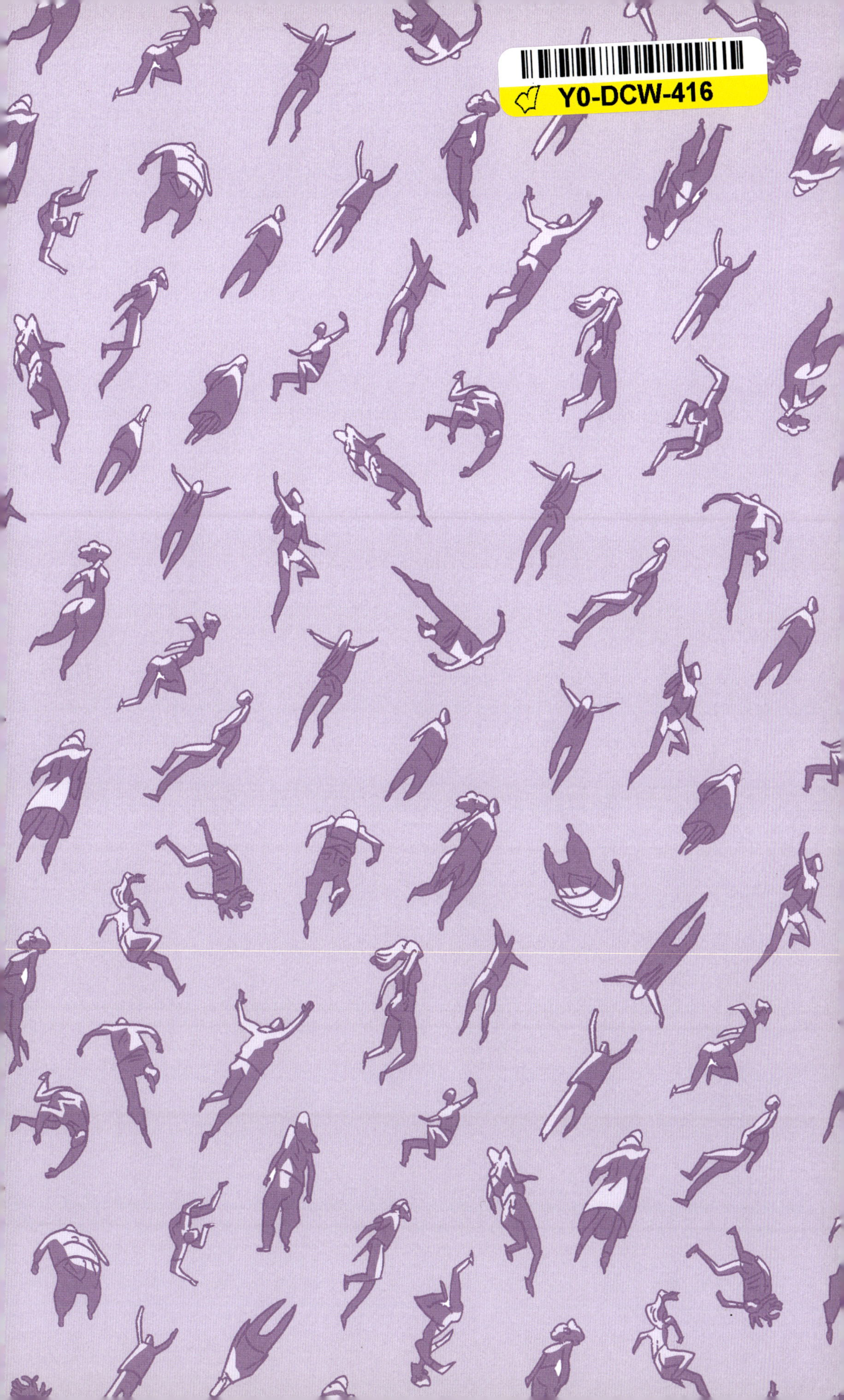

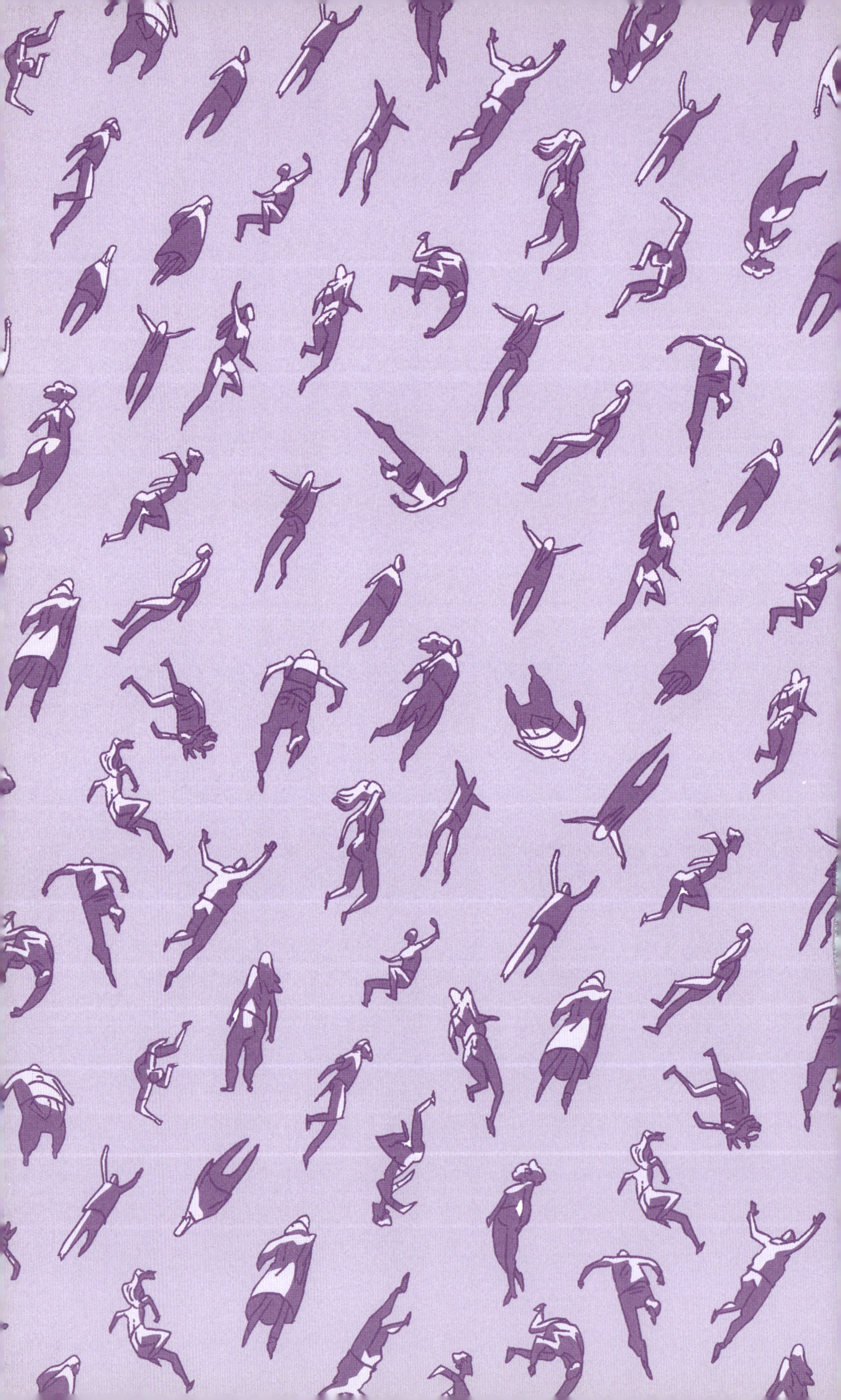

BLACK™ SOLSTICE

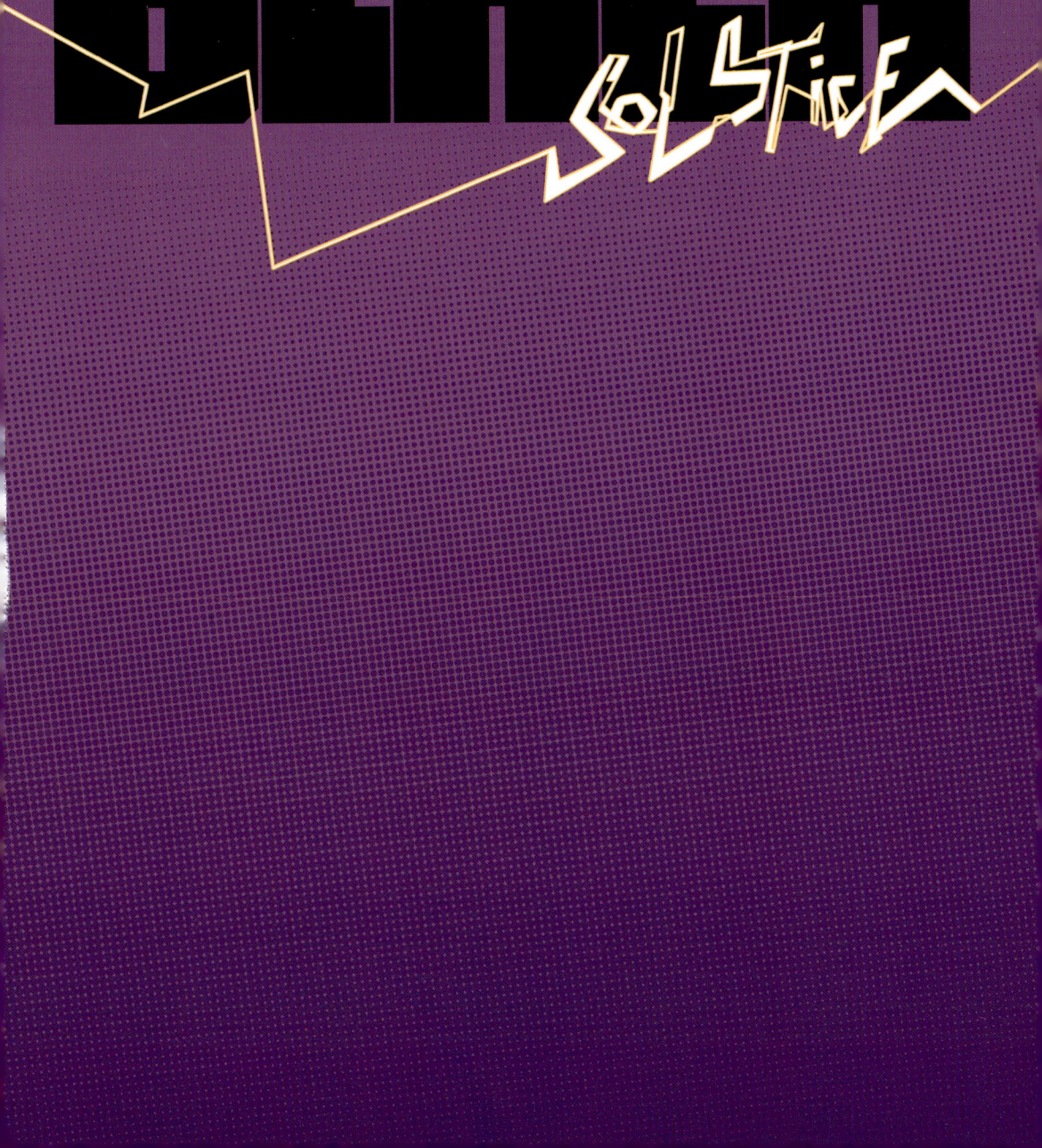

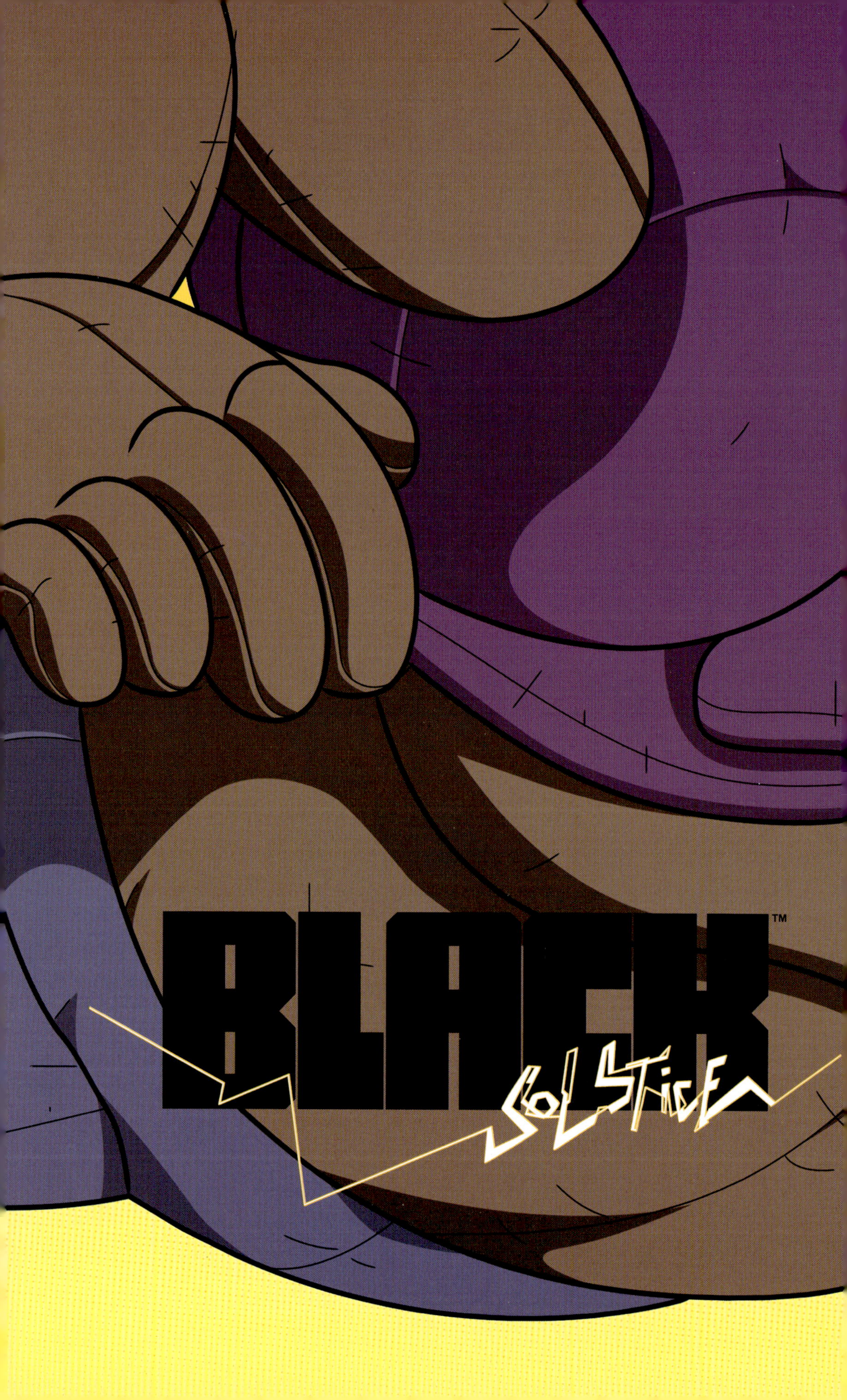
BLACK™
SOLSTICE

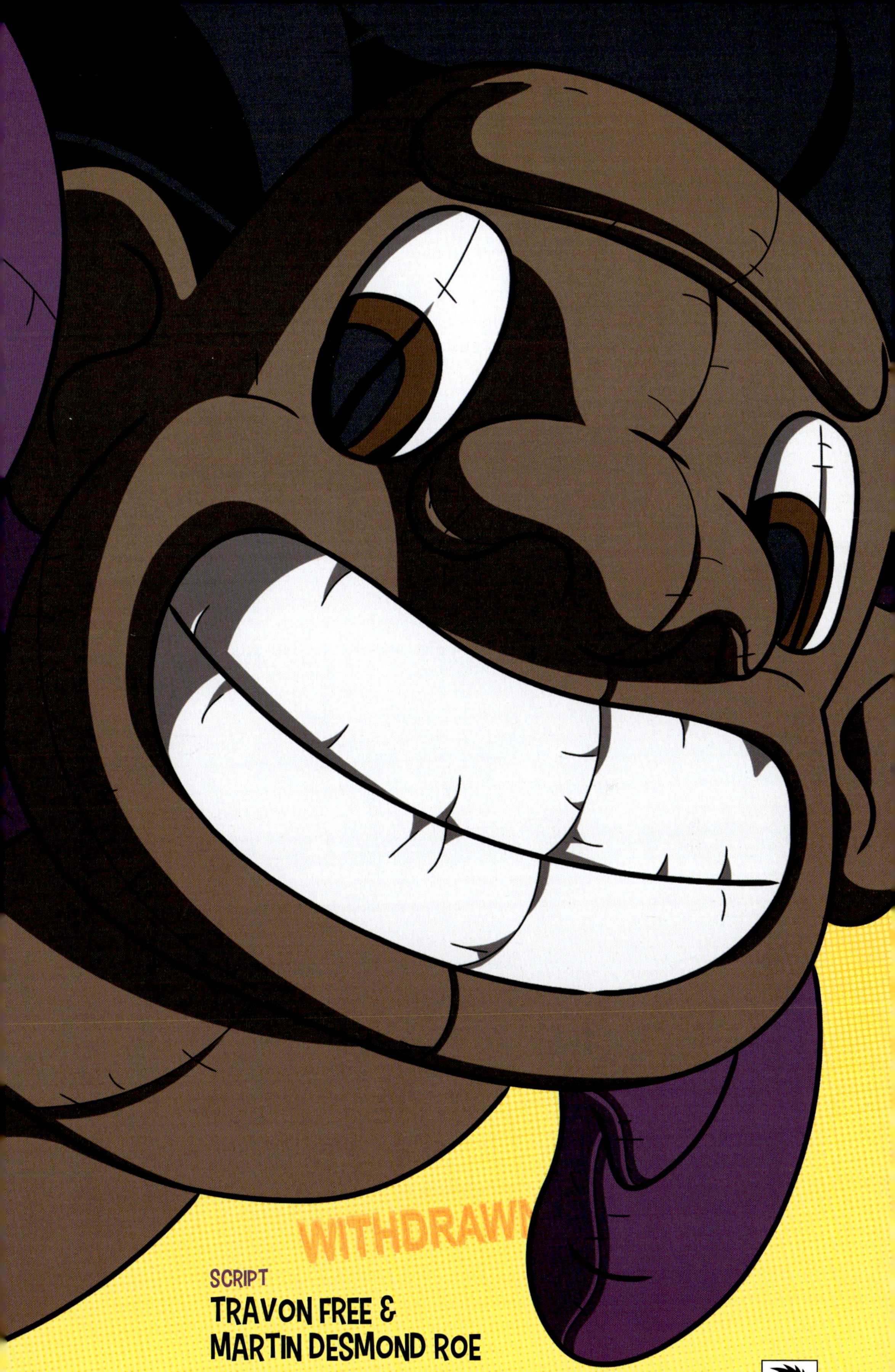

SCRIPT

TRAVON FREE & MARTIN DESMOND ROE

ART, COLORS, LETTERS & COVER

AREMO MASSA

DARK HORSE BOOKS

PRESIDENT & PUBLISHER
MIKE RICHARDSON

EDITOR
MEGAN WALKER

COLLECTION DESIGNER
HANNAH NOBLE

DIGITAL ART TECHNICIAN
ADAM PRUETT

Published by Dark Horse Books
A division of Dark Horse Comics LLC
10956 SE Main Street, Milwaukie, OR 97222
DarkHorse.com

Facebook.com/DarkHorseComics
Twitter.com/DarkHorseComics

First edition: December 2023
Ebook ISBN 978-1-50673-342-5
Hardcover ISBN 978-1-50673-322-7

10 9 8 7 6 5 4 3 2 1

MIX
Paper from
responsible sources
FSC® C169962
FSC
www.fsc.org

Printed in China

INTRODUCTION

You are holding a copy of *Black Solstice*, and for that, we thank you. The journey of *Black Solstice* began on Twitter, long before a bored, transphobic, white-supremacist-enabling, faux-intelligent billionaire came along and killed it. On December 21, 2020, practically every Black person on Twitter started declaring, completely spontaneously, what superpower they were going to get on the day of the winter solstice.

For us it was an amazing day, one of those moments that remind you why you love the internet, where each post was cleverer than the last and every emotional beat you could think of was hit, from hilarious to disturbing to profound.

It felt like magic, and it kind of was. Because in putting together this book, we traced the idea back to its origin and after a lot of digging it turned out . . . there really wasn't one. There was no plan. No brand behind it. No viral marketing. Not even a clear or definitive starting point.

Instead, it kind of formed piece by piece, bouncing from tweet to tweet, and from sincerity to irony in the weeks leading up to the solstice, dumping joy all over the timeline for everyone and proving, once again, that Black Twitter is the most creative place in the known universe.

Ultimately, with this book we tried to capture the fun and excitement of that explosive creativity and turn it into a story that explores why Black people dream so deeply of these superpowers, or any power at all for that matter, and what they would do with that power, if it was actually obtained.

We hope you enjoy the ride that is *Black Solstice* and that if this ever really does happen, that every Black person gets the most amazing superpower. Except Clarence Thomas. **Fuck that guy.**

–TRAVON FREE & MARTIN DESMOND ROE

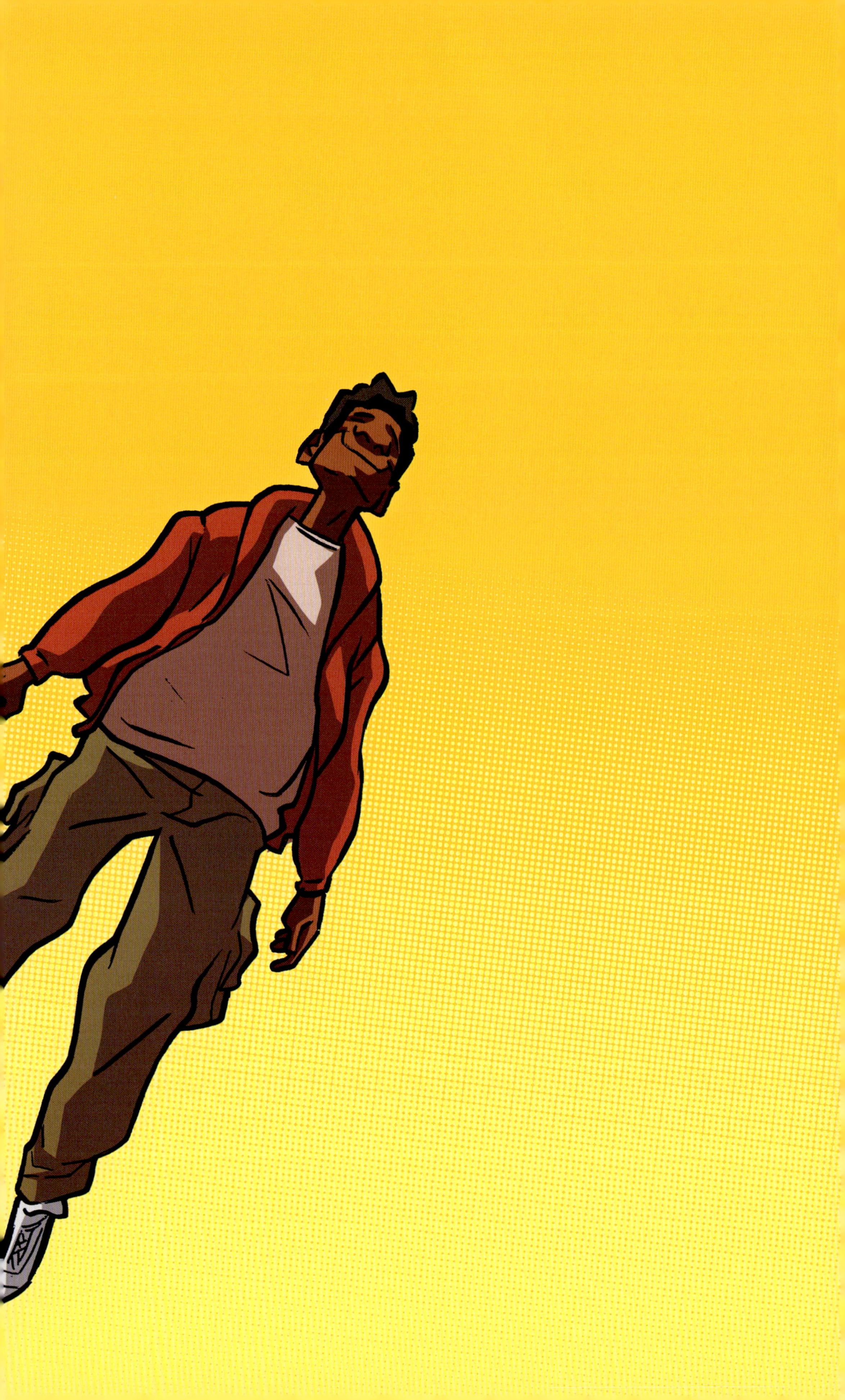

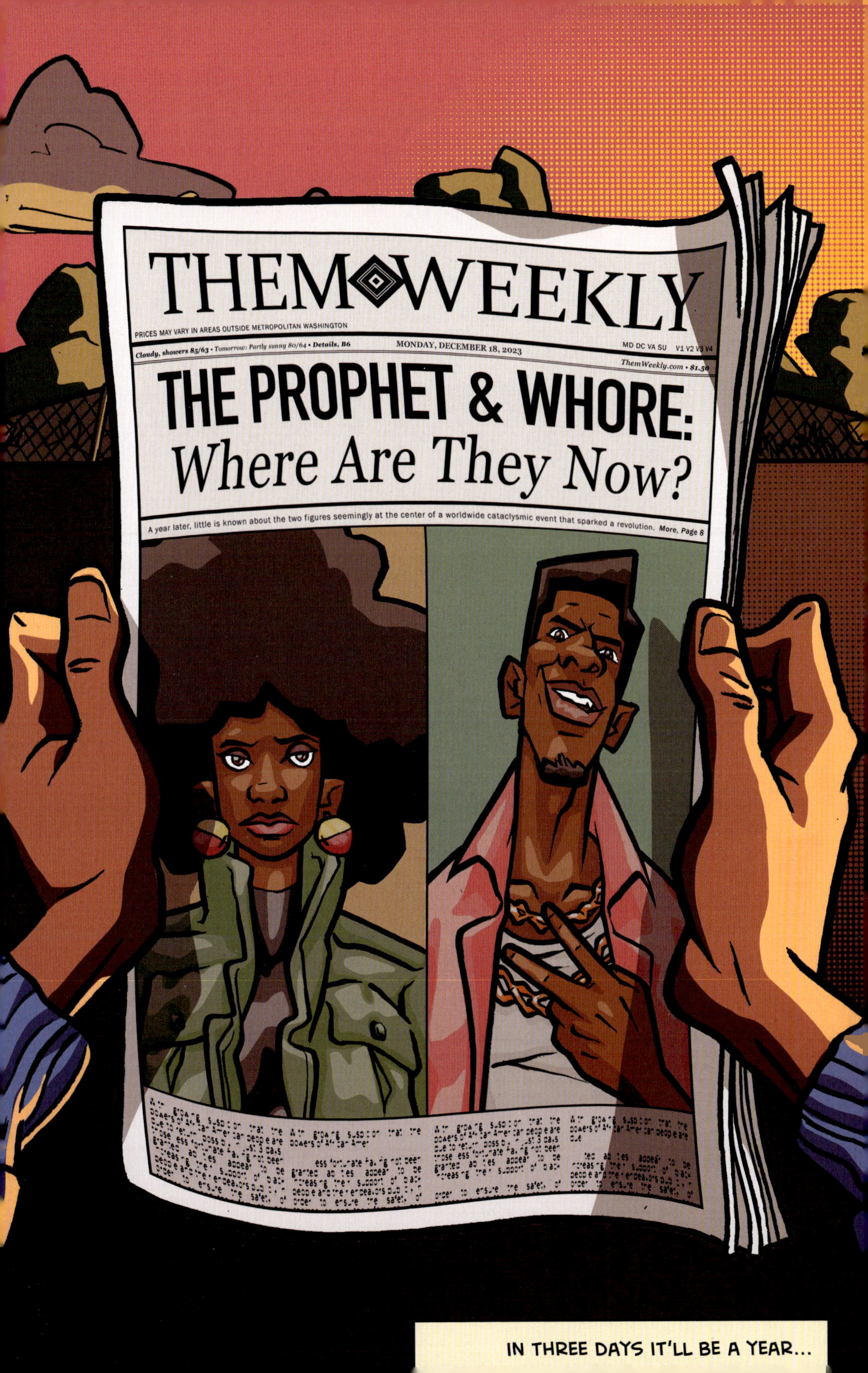
THEM WEEKLY
PRICES MAY VARY IN AREAS OUTSIDE METROPOLITAN WASHINGTON
Cloudy, showers 85/63 • Tomorrow: Partly sunny 80/64 • Details, B6
MONDAY, DECEMBER 18, 2023
MD DC VA SU V1 V2 V3 V4
ThemWeekly.com • $1.50
THE PROPHET & WHORE:
Where Are They Now?
A year later, little is known about the two figures seemingly at the center of a worldwide cataclysmic event that sparked a revolution. More, Page 8
IN THREE DAYS IT'LL BE A YEAR...

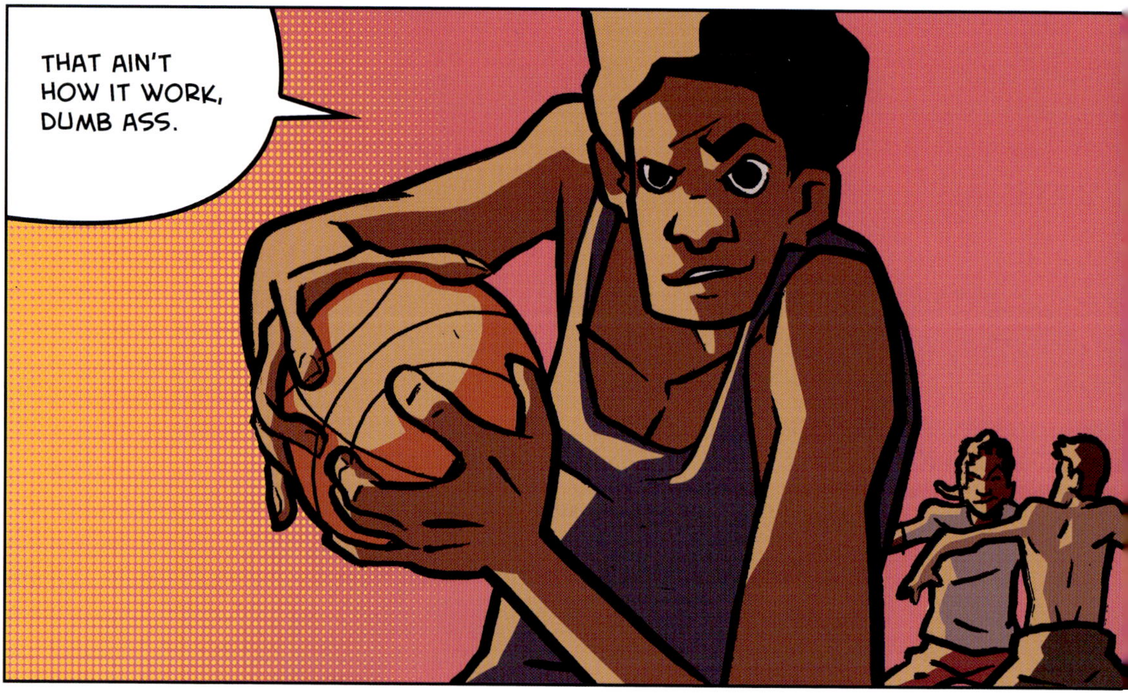
THAT AIN'T HOW IT WORK, DUMB ASS.

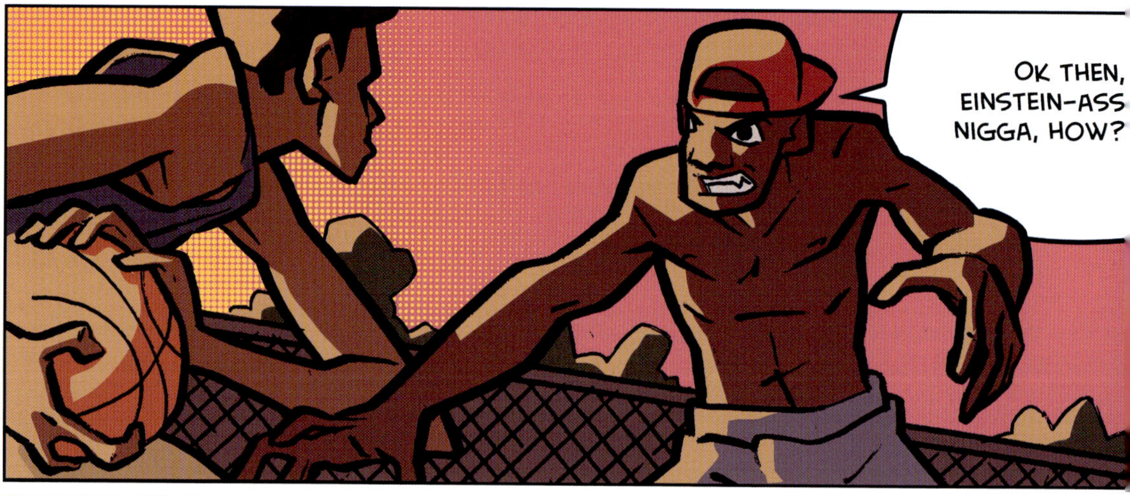
OK THEN, EINSTEIN-ASS NIGGA, HOW?

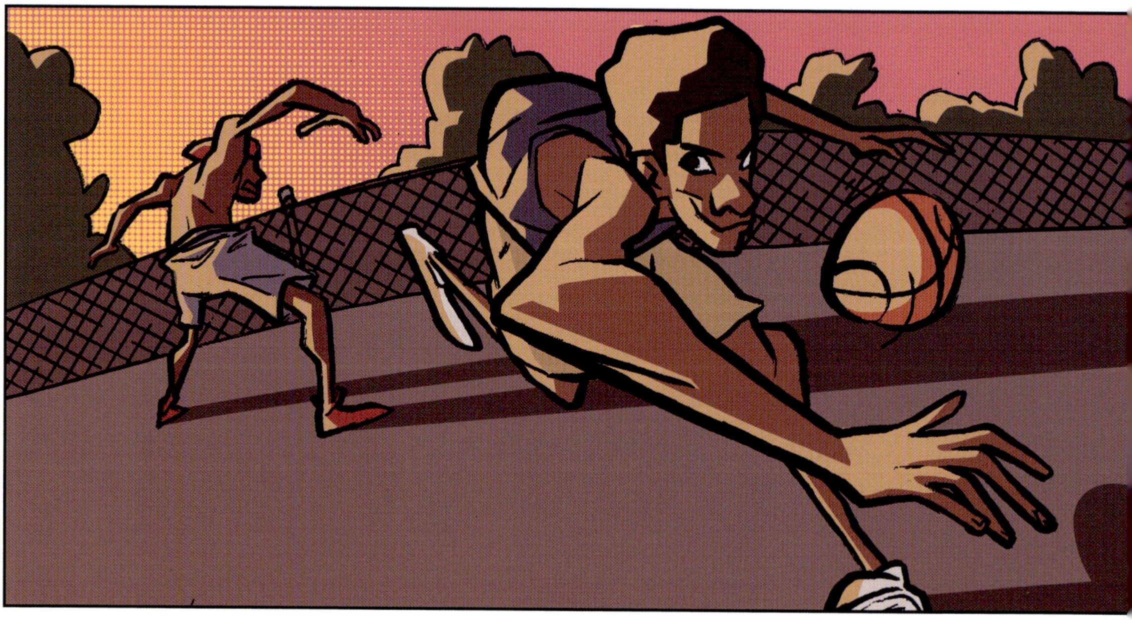

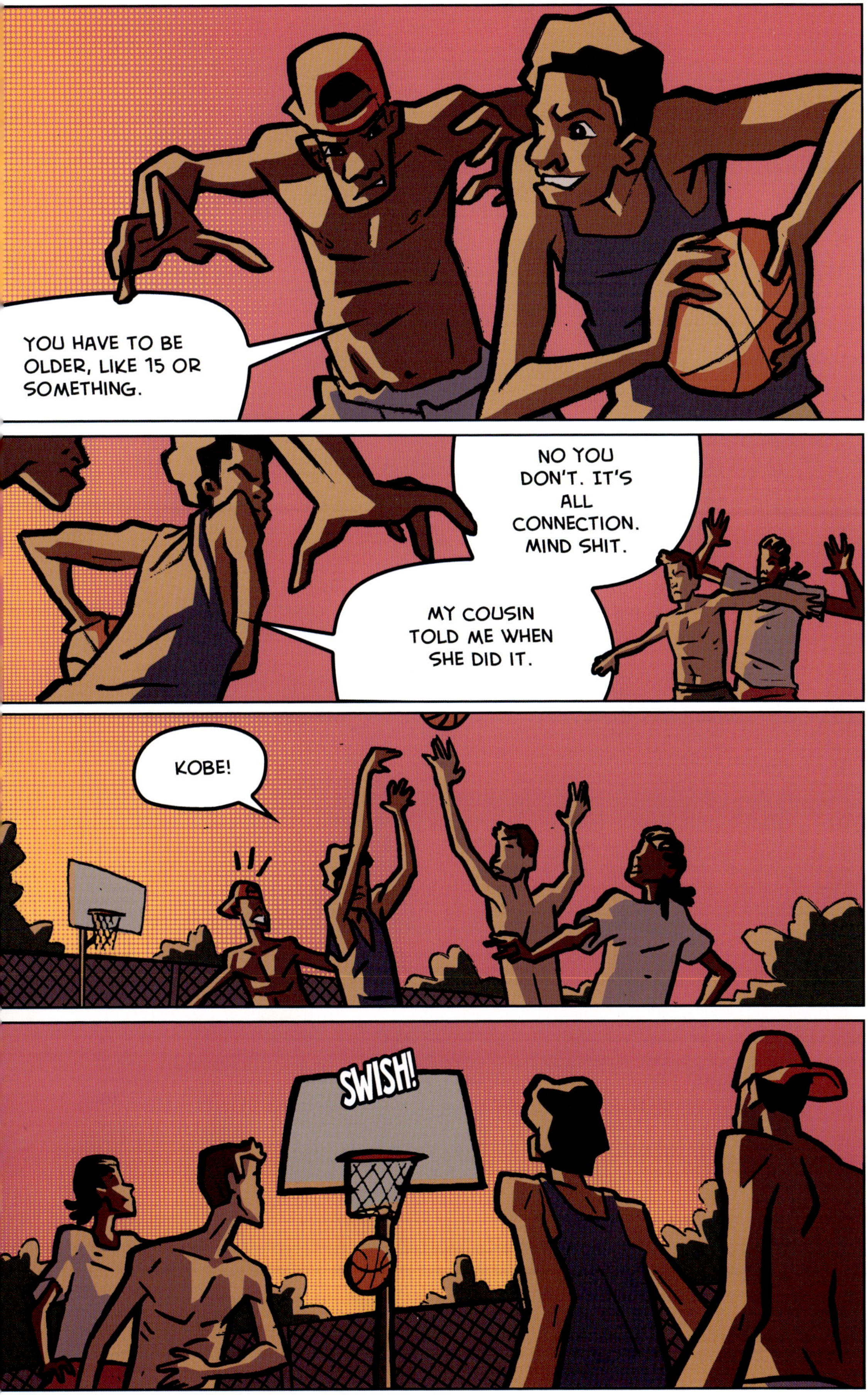
YOU HAVE TO BE OLDER, LIKE 15 OR SOMETHING.
NO YOU DON'T. IT'S ALL CONNECTION. MIND SHIT.
MY COUSIN TOLD ME WHEN SHE DID IT.
KOBE!
SWISH!

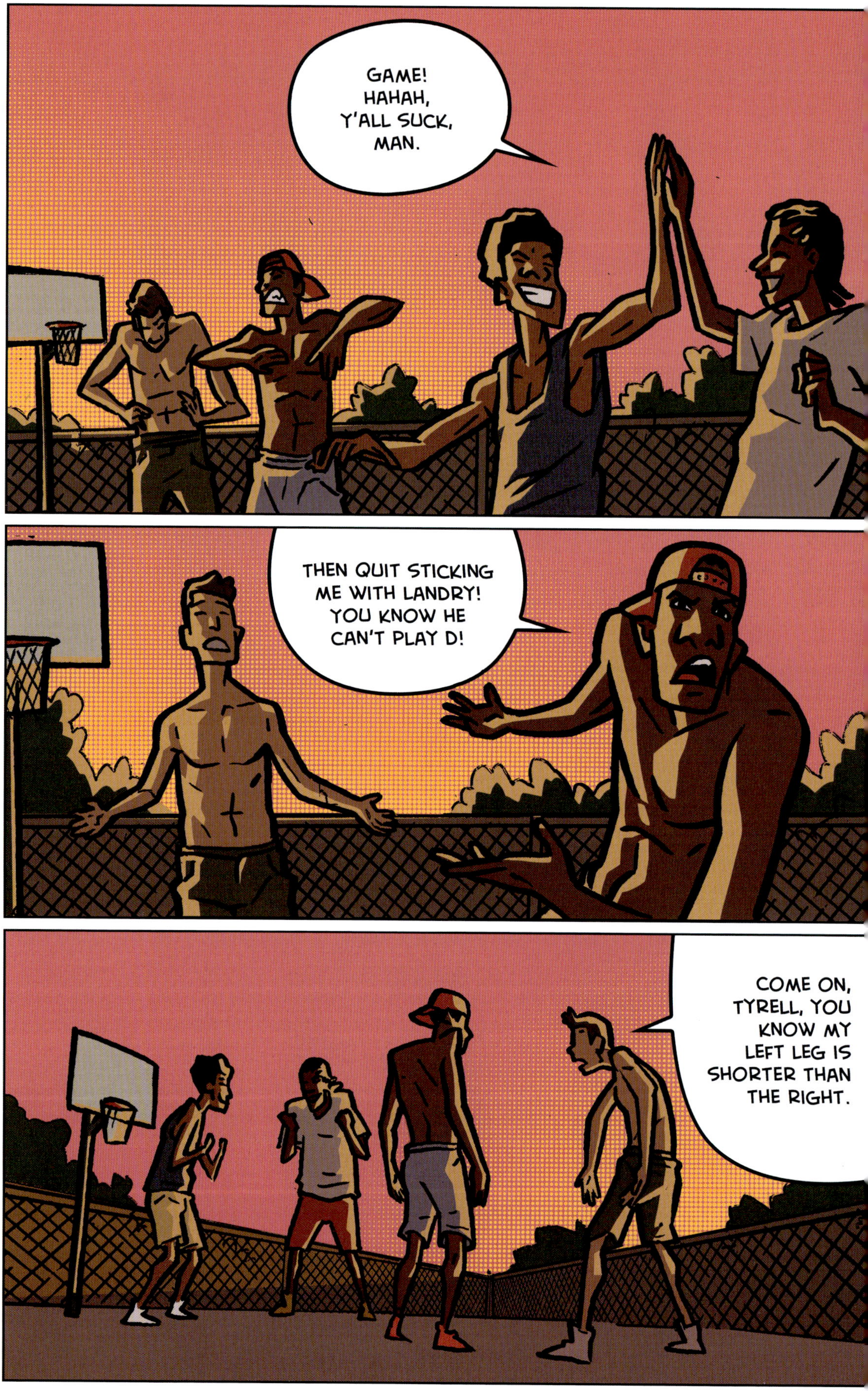
GAME! HAHAH, Y'ALL SUCK, MAN.
THEN QUIT STICKING ME WITH LANDRY! YOU KNOW HE CAN'T PLAY D!
COME ON, TYRELL, YOU KNOW MY LEFT LEG IS SHORTER THAN THE RIGHT.

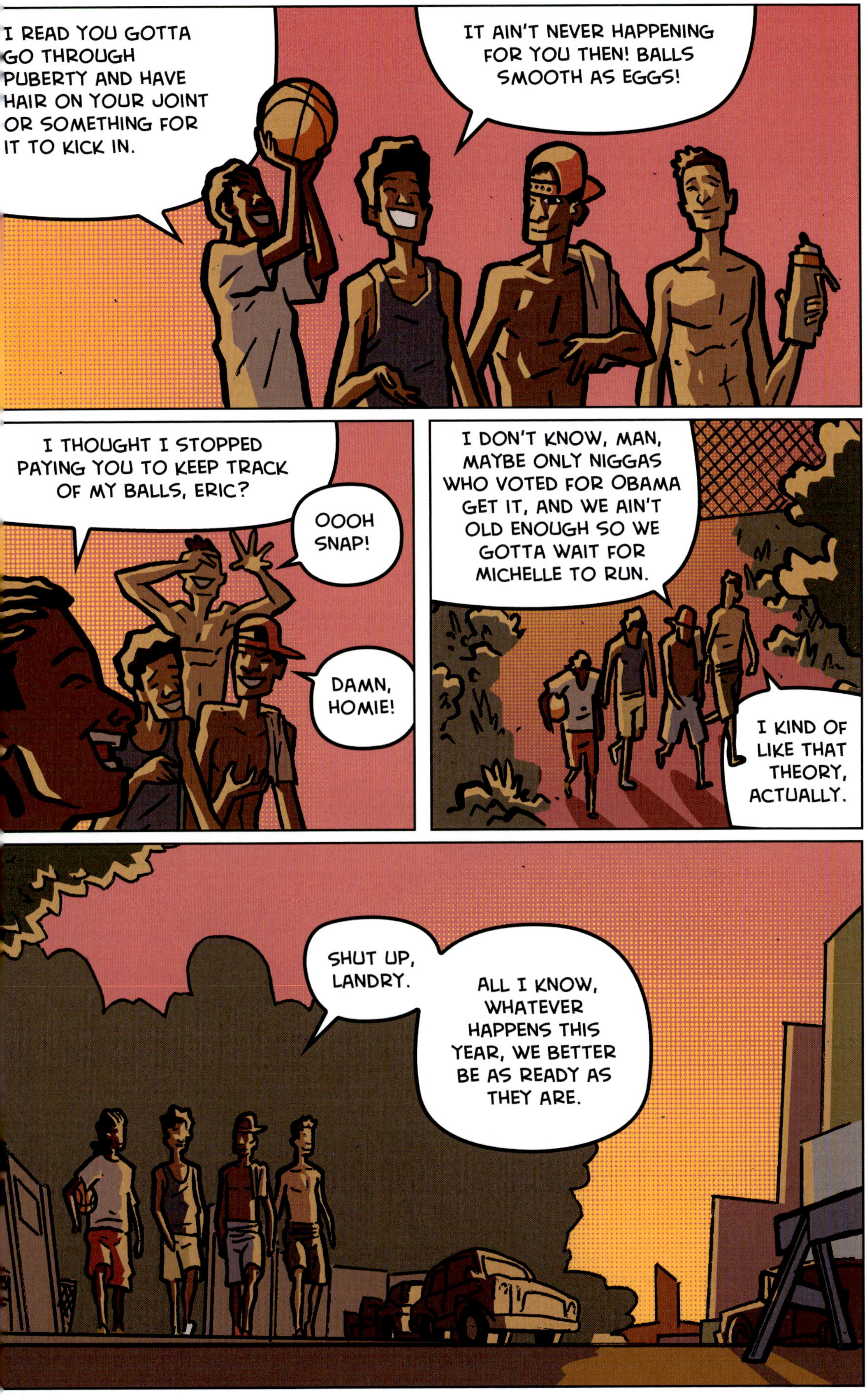
I READ YOU GOTTA GO THROUGH PUBERTY AND HAVE HAIR ON YOUR JOINT OR SOMETHING FOR IT TO KICK IN.
IT AIN'T NEVER HAPPENING FOR YOU THEN! BALLS SMOOTH AS EGGS!
I THOUGHT I STOPPED PAYING YOU TO KEEP TRACK OF MY BALLS, ERIC?
OOOH SNAP!
DAMN, HOMIE!
I DON'T KNOW, MAN, MAYBE ONLY NIGGAS WHO VOTED FOR OBAMA GET IT, AND WE AIN'T OLD ENOUGH SO WE GOTTA WAIT FOR MICHELLE TO RUN.
I KIND OF LIKE THAT THEORY, ACTUALLY.
SHUT UP, LANDRY.
ALL I KNOW, WHATEVER HAPPENS THIS YEAR, WE BETTER BE AS READY AS THEY ARE.

AND IN THREE DAYS IT WILL HAPPEN AGAIN.
I WONDER IF WHITE PEOPLE WILL GET IT THIS TIME?

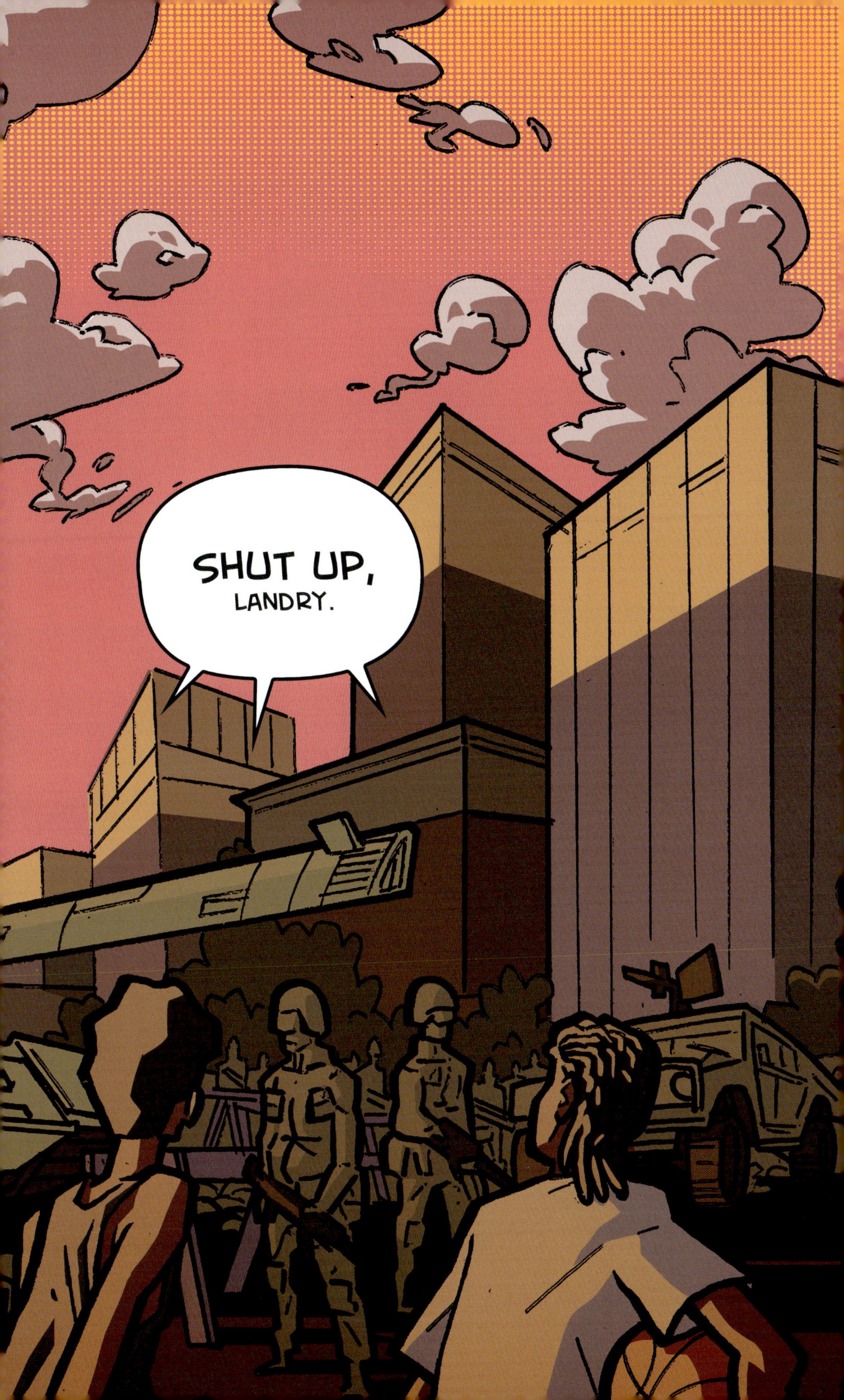
SHUT UP,
LANDRY.

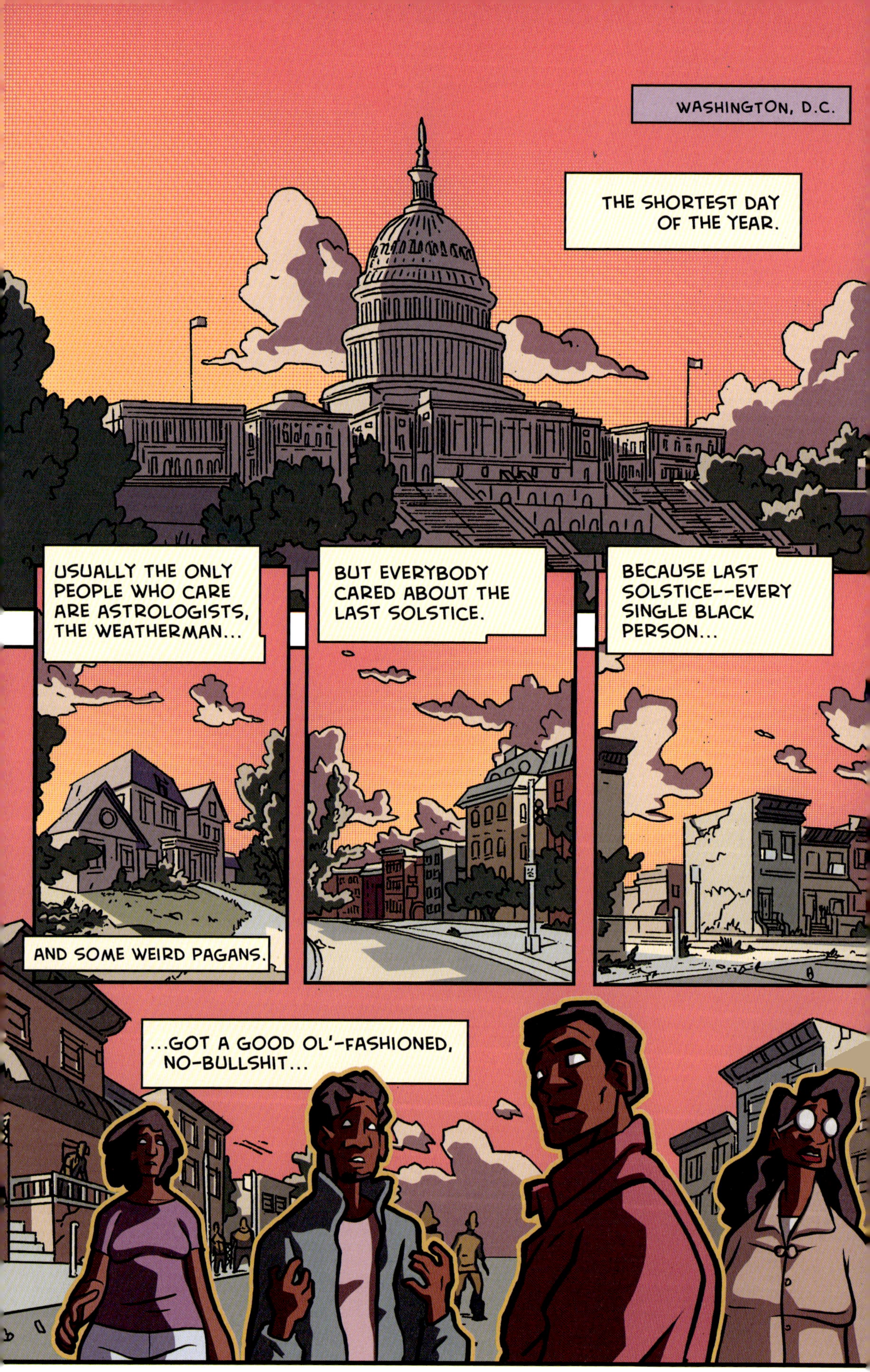
WASHINGTON, D.C.
THE SHORTEST DAY OF THE YEAR.
USUALLY THE ONLY PEOPLE WHO CARE ARE ASTROLOGISTS, THE WEATHERMAN...
AND SOME WEIRD PAGANS.
BUT EVERYBODY CARED ABOUT THE LAST SOLSTICE.
BECAUSE LAST SOLSTICE--EVERY SINGLE BLACK PERSON...
...GOT A GOOD OL'-FASHIONED, NO-BULLSHIT...

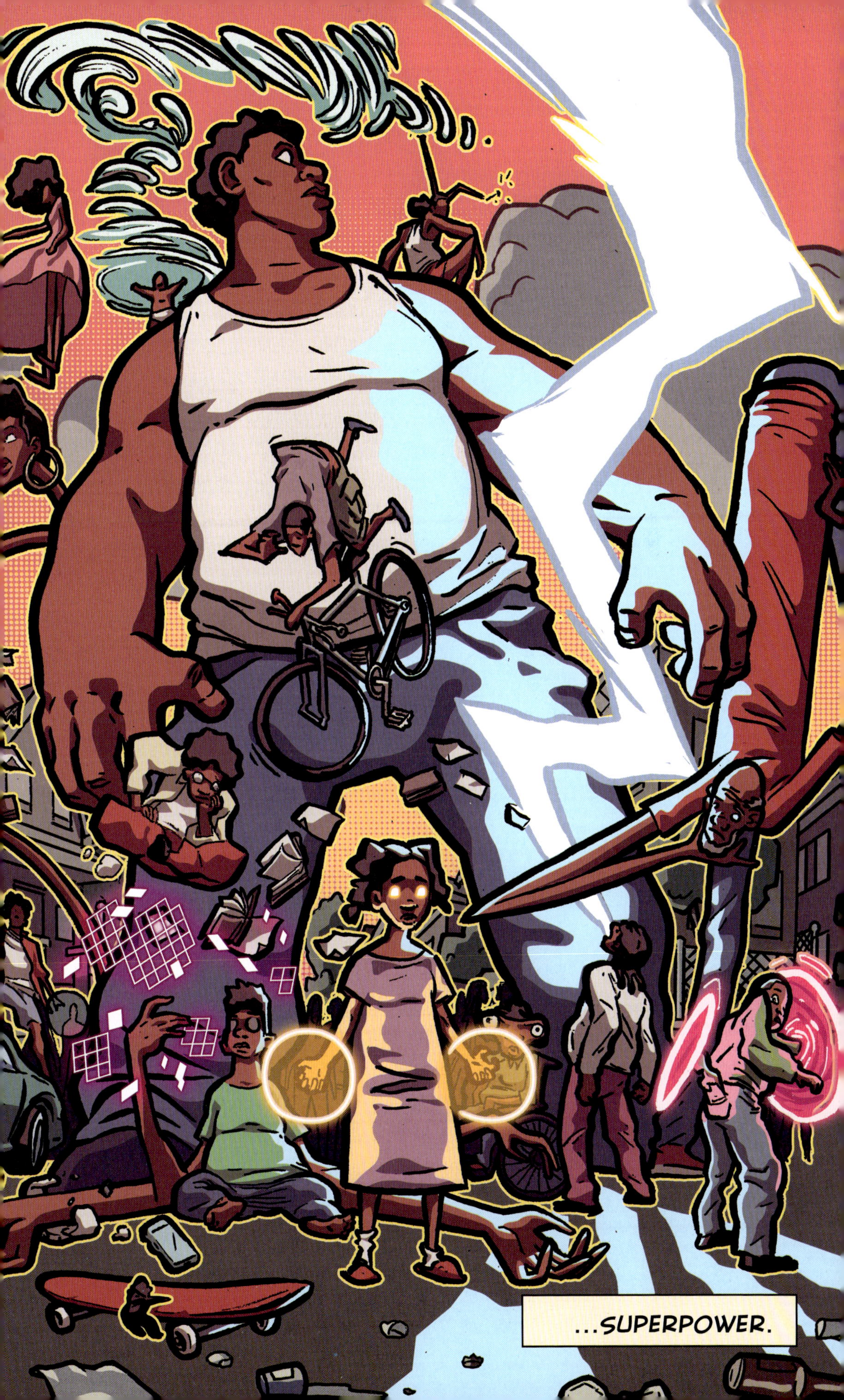
...SUPERPOWER.

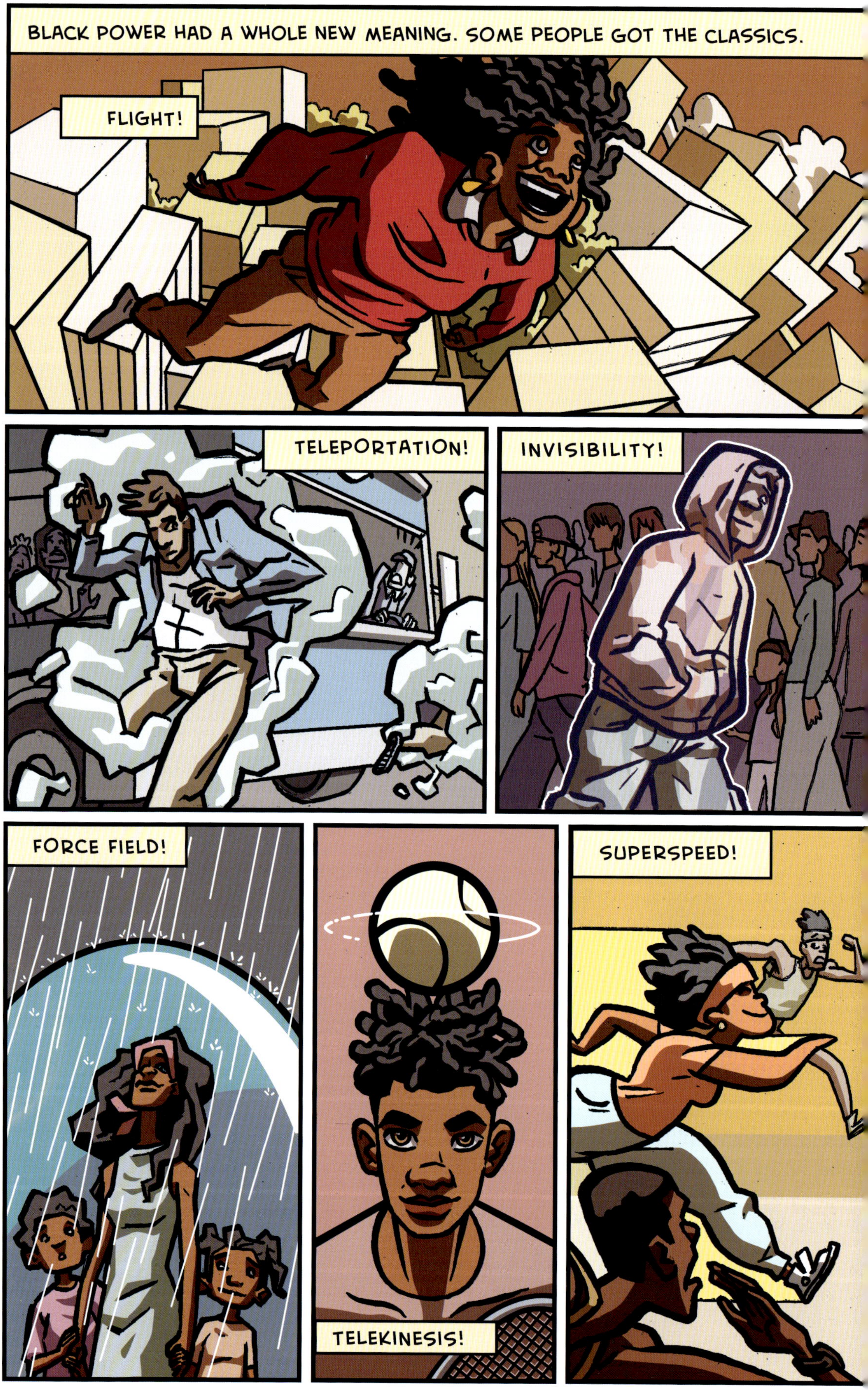
BLACK POWER HAD A WHOLE NEW MEANING. SOME PEOPLE GOT THE CLASSICS.
FLIGHT!
TELEPORTATION!
INVISIBILITY!
FORCE FIELD!
TELEKINESIS!
SUPERSPEED!

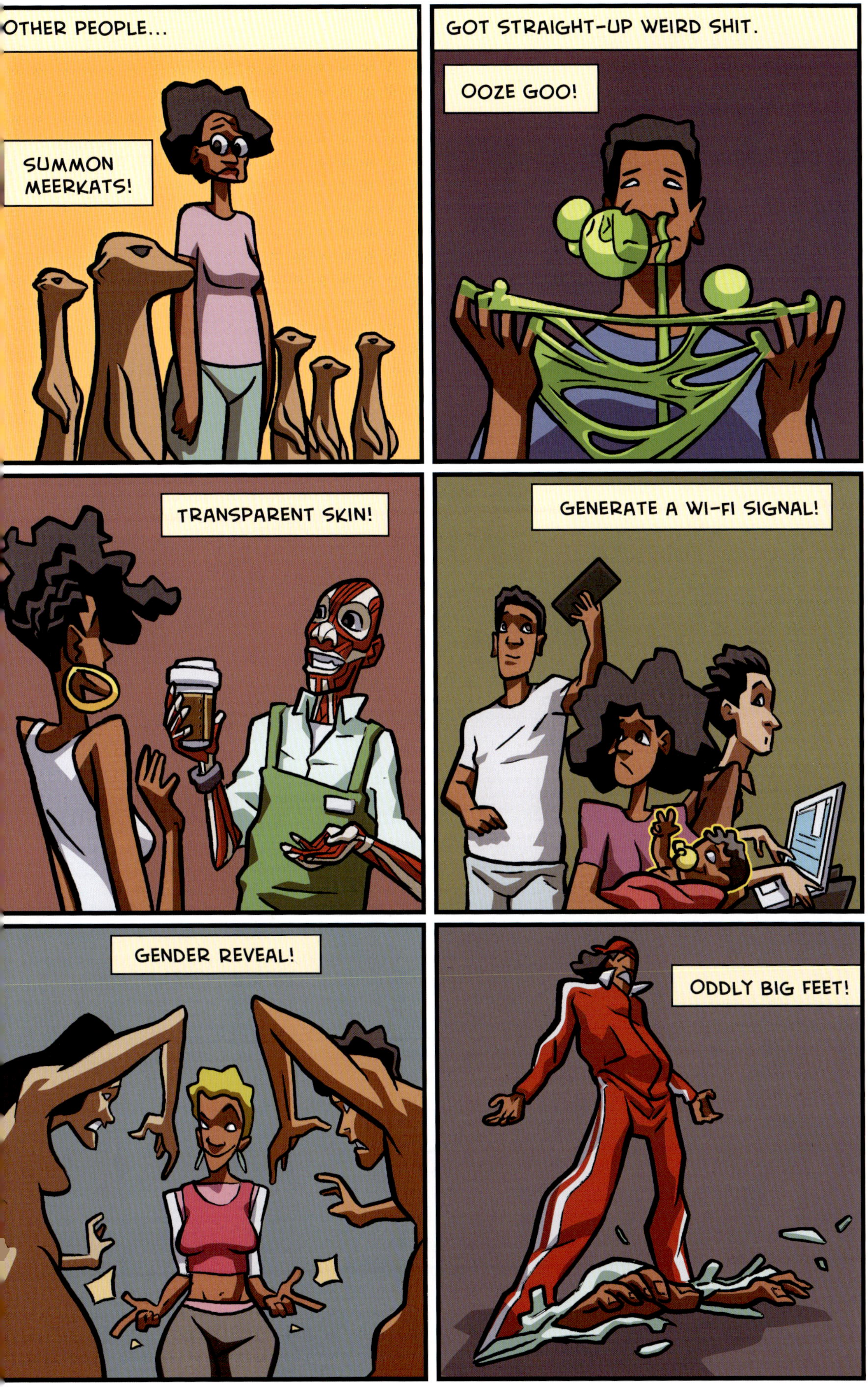
OTHER PEOPLE...
SUMMON MEERKATS!
GOT STRAIGHT-UP WEIRD SHIT.
OOZE GOO!
TRANSPARENT SKIN!
GENERATE A WI-FI SIGNAL!
GENDER REVEAL!
ODDLY BIG FEET!

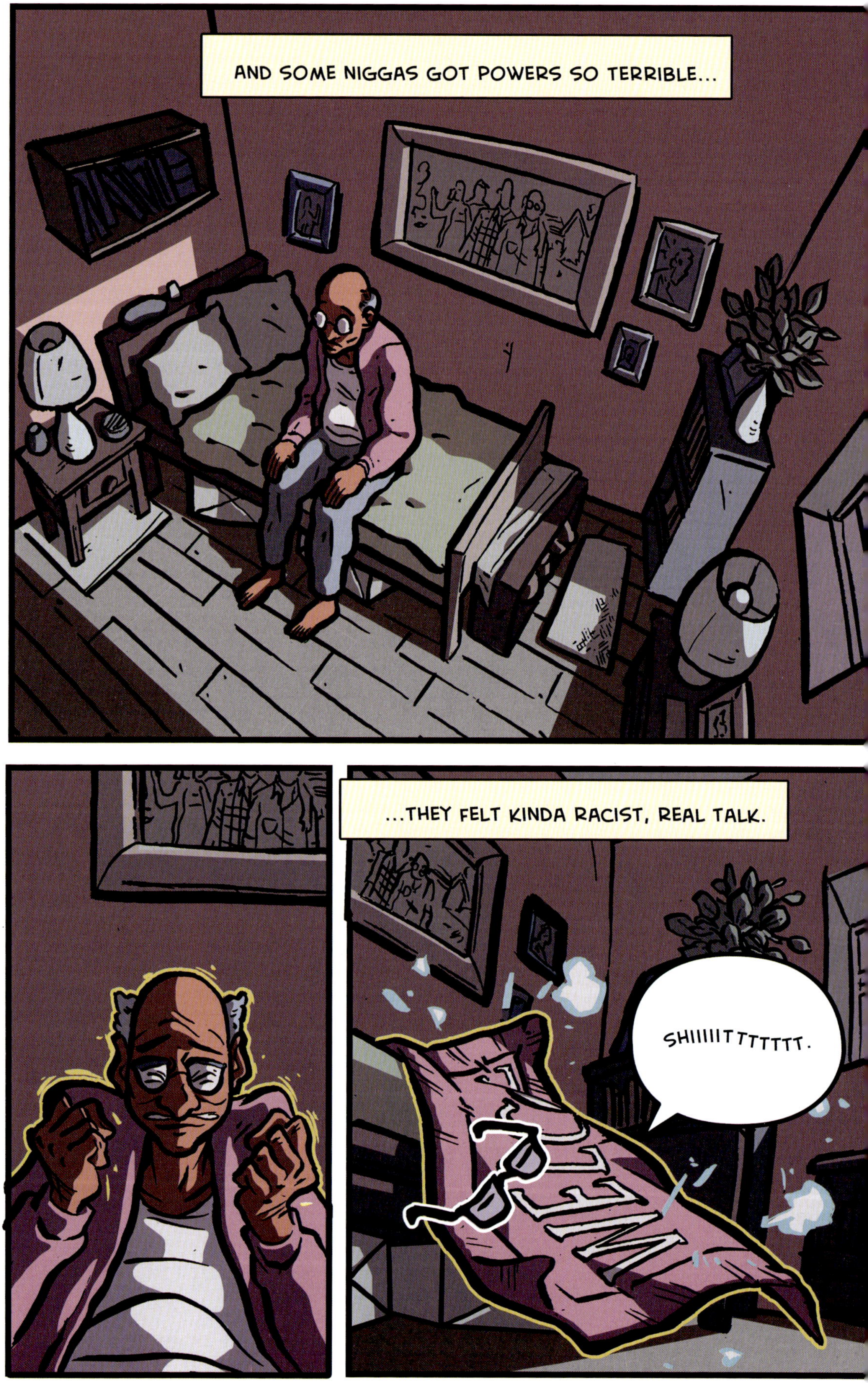
AND SOME NIGGAS GOT POWERS SO TERRIBLE...
...THEY FELT KINDA RACIST, REAL TALK.
SHIIIIITTTTTTT.

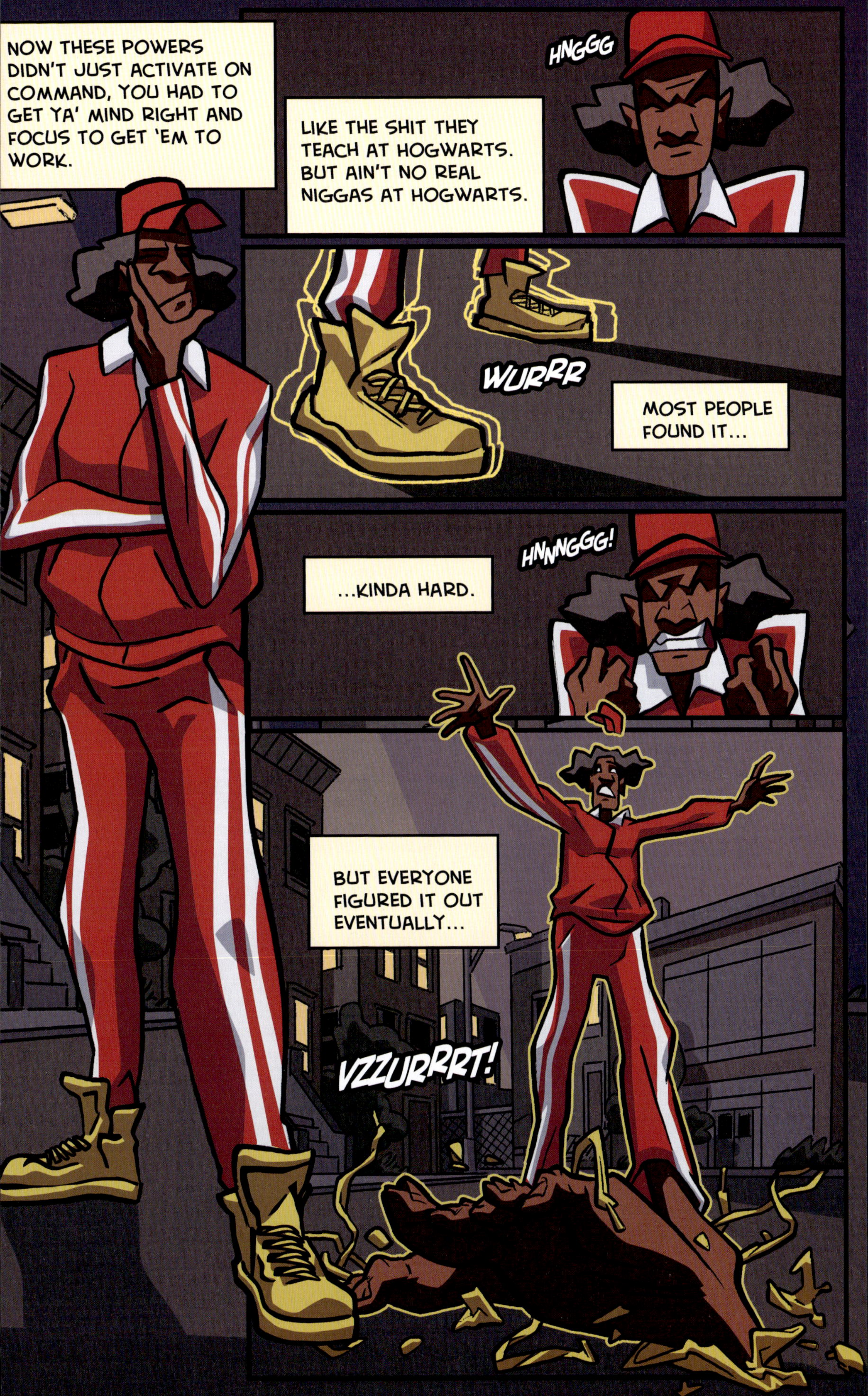
NOW THESE POWERS DIDN'T JUST ACTIVATE ON COMMAND, YOU HAD TO GET YA' MIND RIGHT AND FOCUS TO GET 'EM TO WORK.
LIKE THE SHIT THEY TEACH AT HOGWARTS. BUT AIN'T NO REAL NIGGAS AT HOGWARTS.
HNGGG
WURRR
MOST PEOPLE FOUND IT...
...KINDA HARD.
HNNNGGG!
BUT EVERYONE FIGURED IT OUT EVENTUALLY...
VZZURRRT!

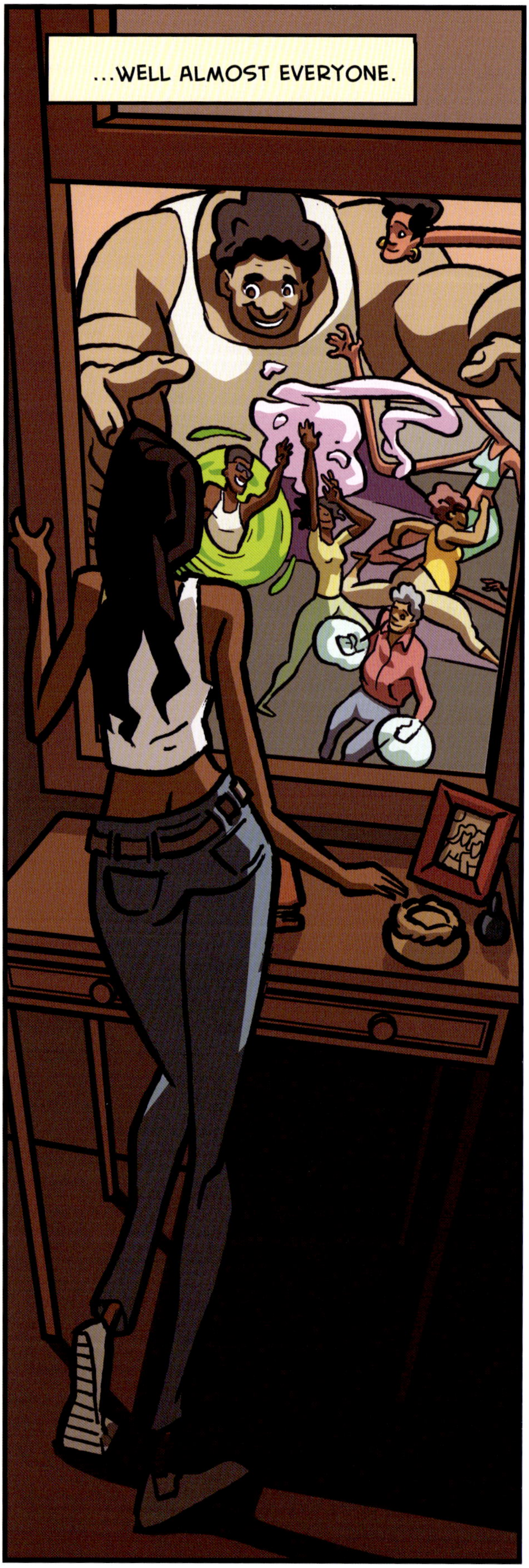
...WELL ALMOST EVERYONE.

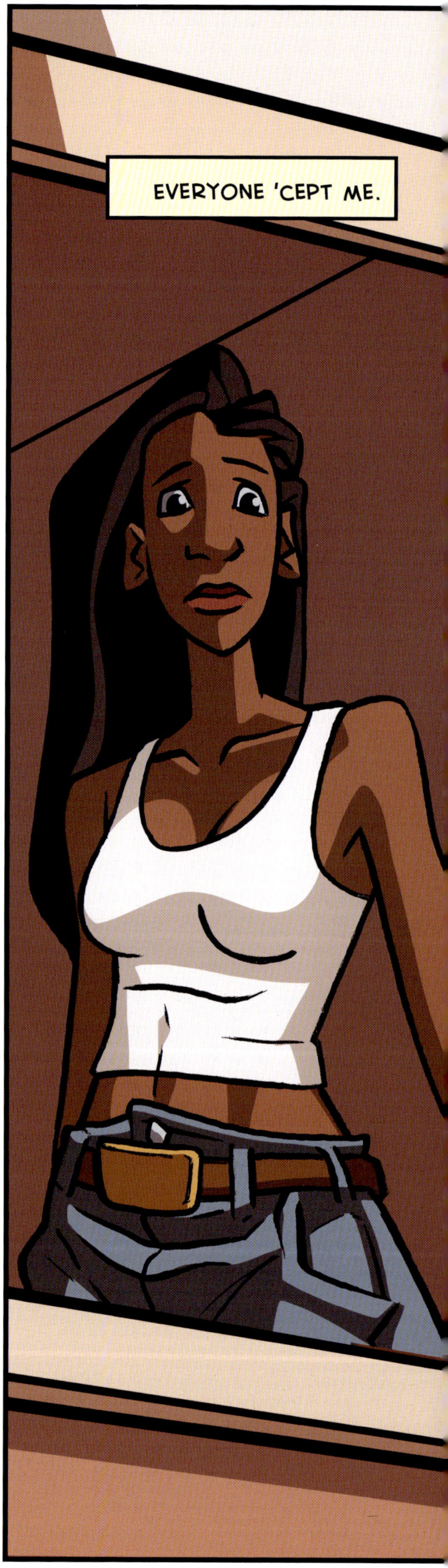
EVERYONE 'CEPT ME.

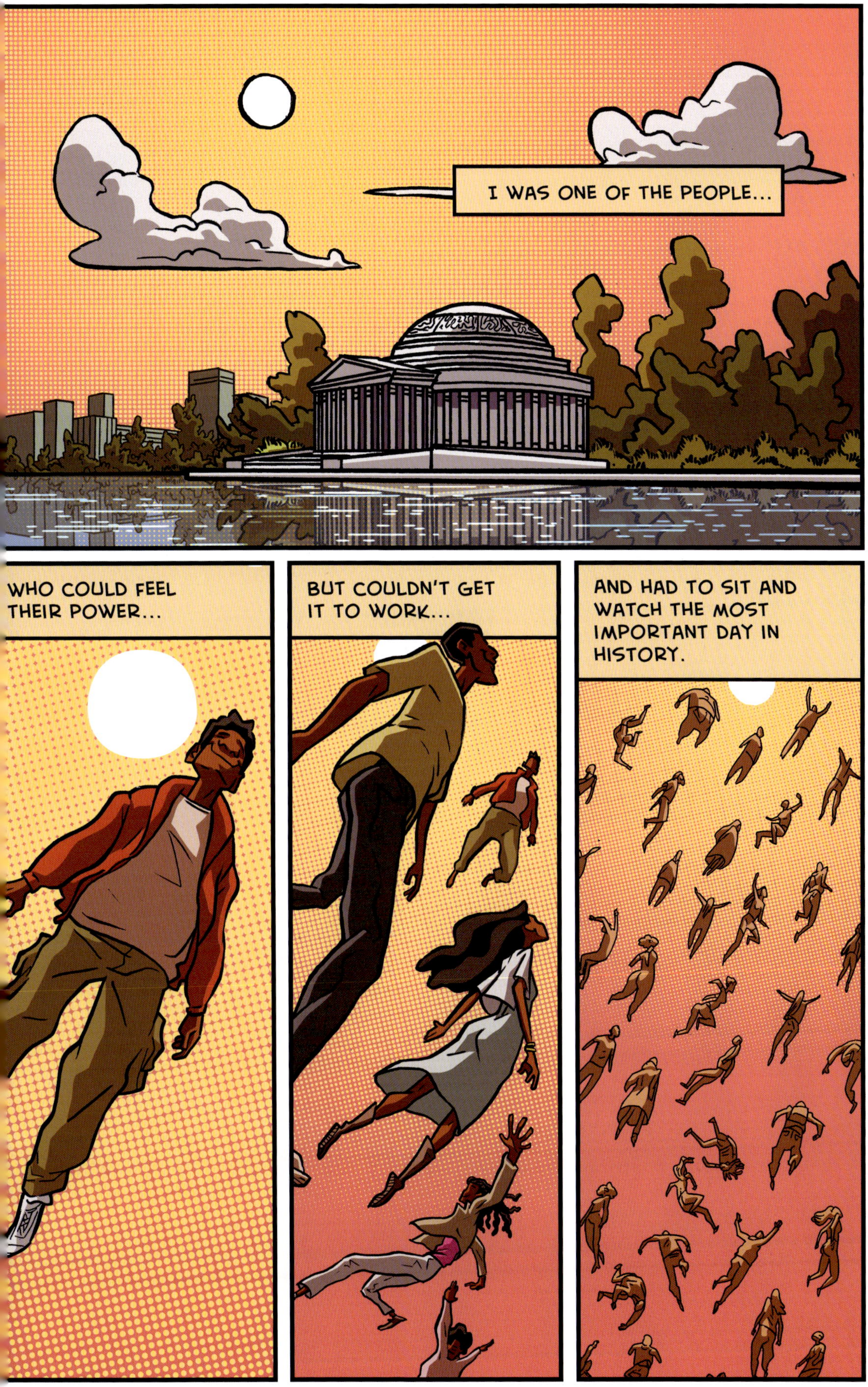
I WAS ONE OF THE PEOPLE...
WHO COULD FEEL THEIR POWER...
BUT COULDN'T GET IT TO WORK...
AND HAD TO SIT AND WATCH THE MOST IMPORTANT DAY IN HISTORY.

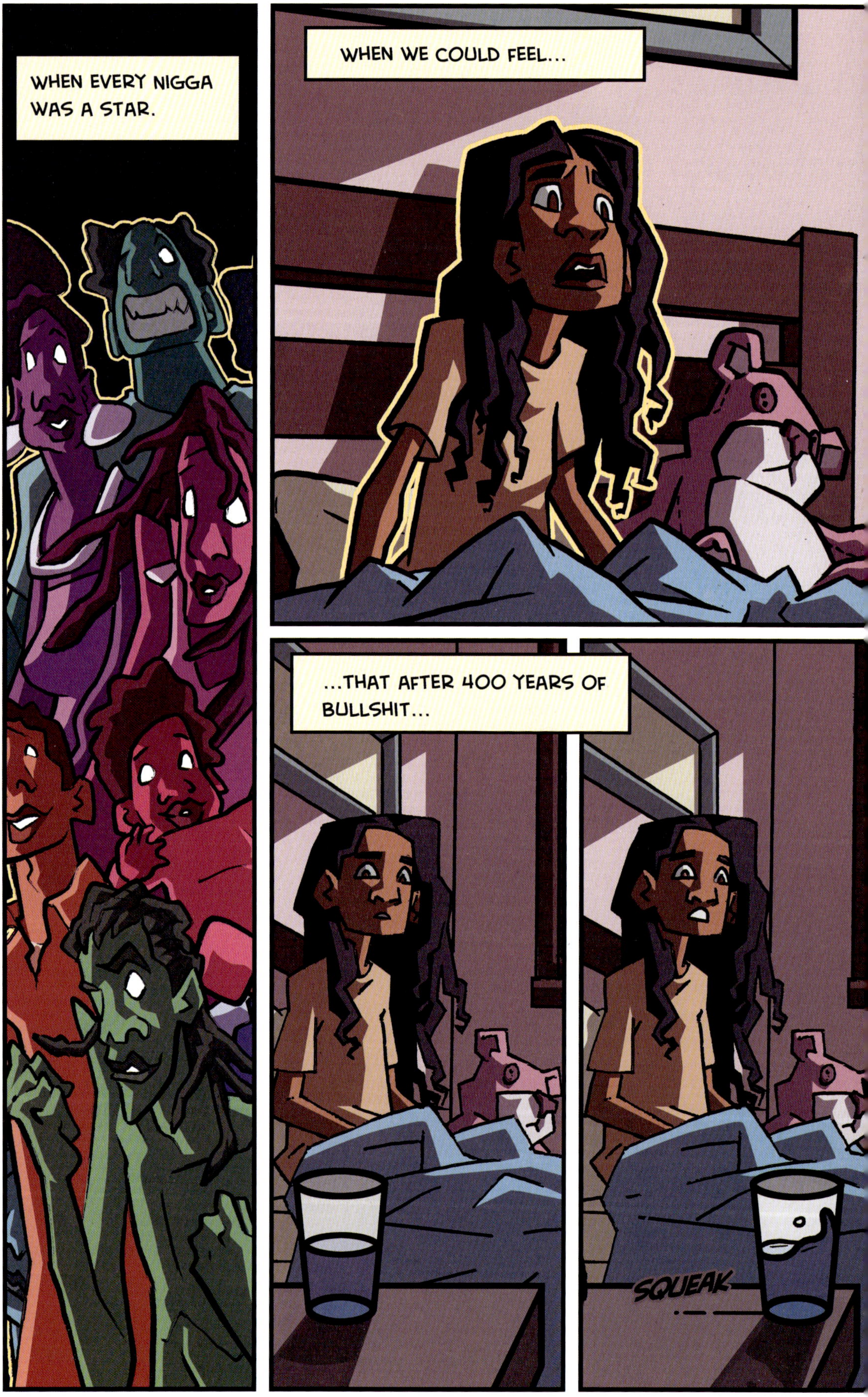
WHEN EVERY NIGGA WAS A STAR.
WHEN WE COULD FEEL...
...THAT AFTER 400 YEARS OF BULLSHIT...
SQUEAK

...WE FINALLY HAD THE POWER...
WATER SUPPLY
CITY OF FINT
...TO CHANGE THE WORLD.

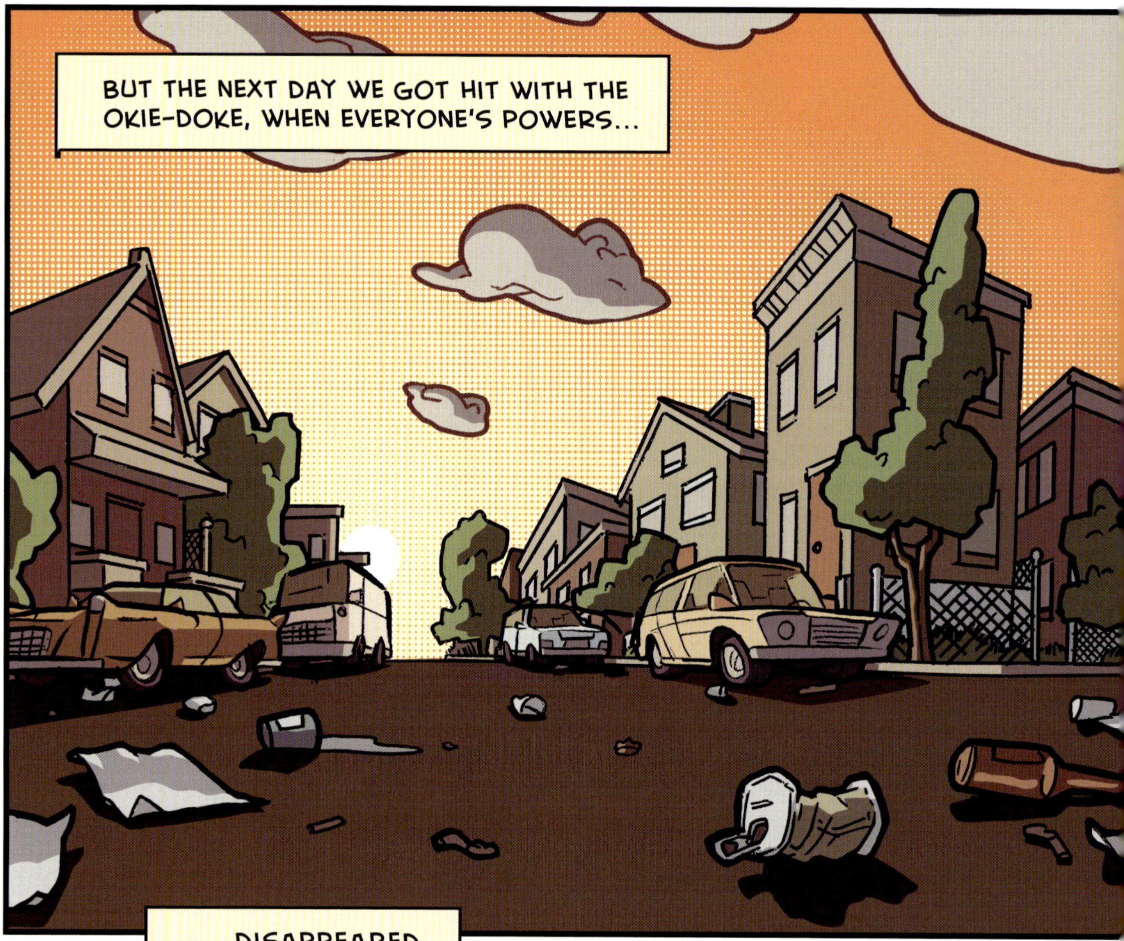
BUT THE NEXT DAY WE GOT HIT WITH THE OKIE-DOKE, WHEN EVERYONE'S POWERS...
...DISAPPEARED.

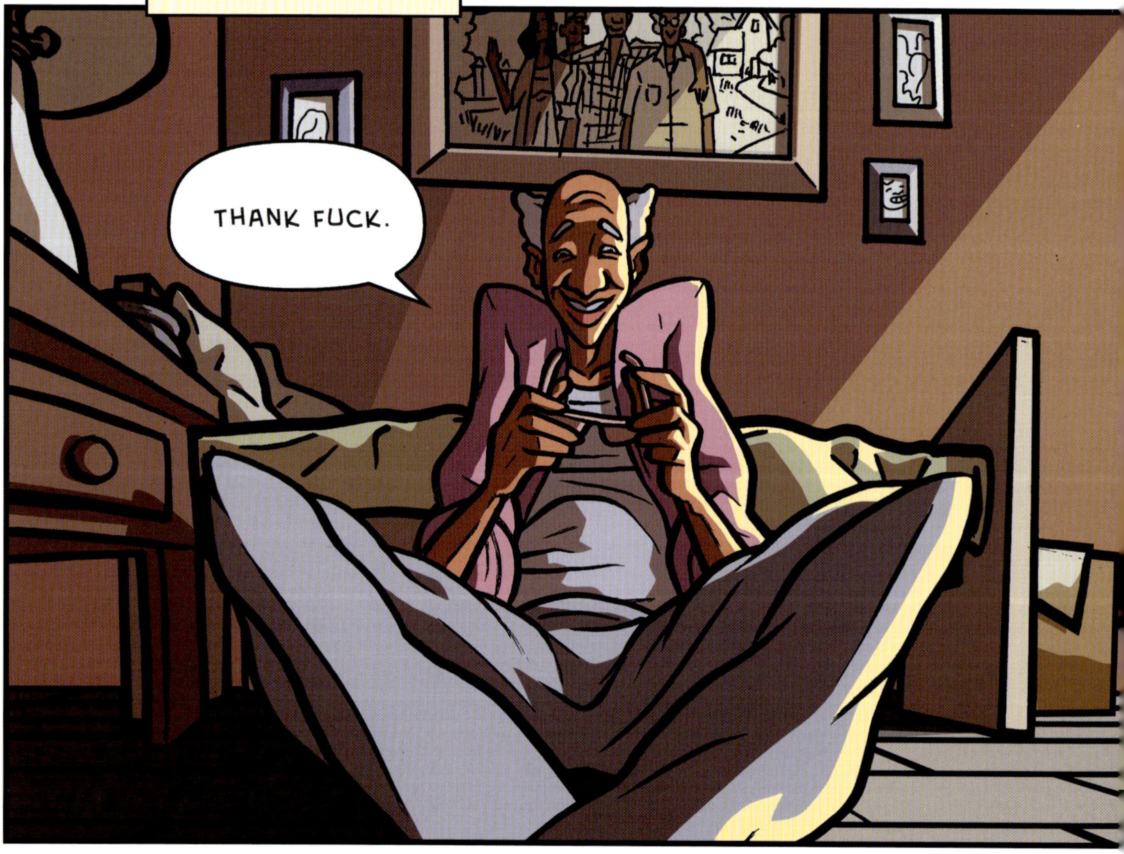
THANK FUCK.

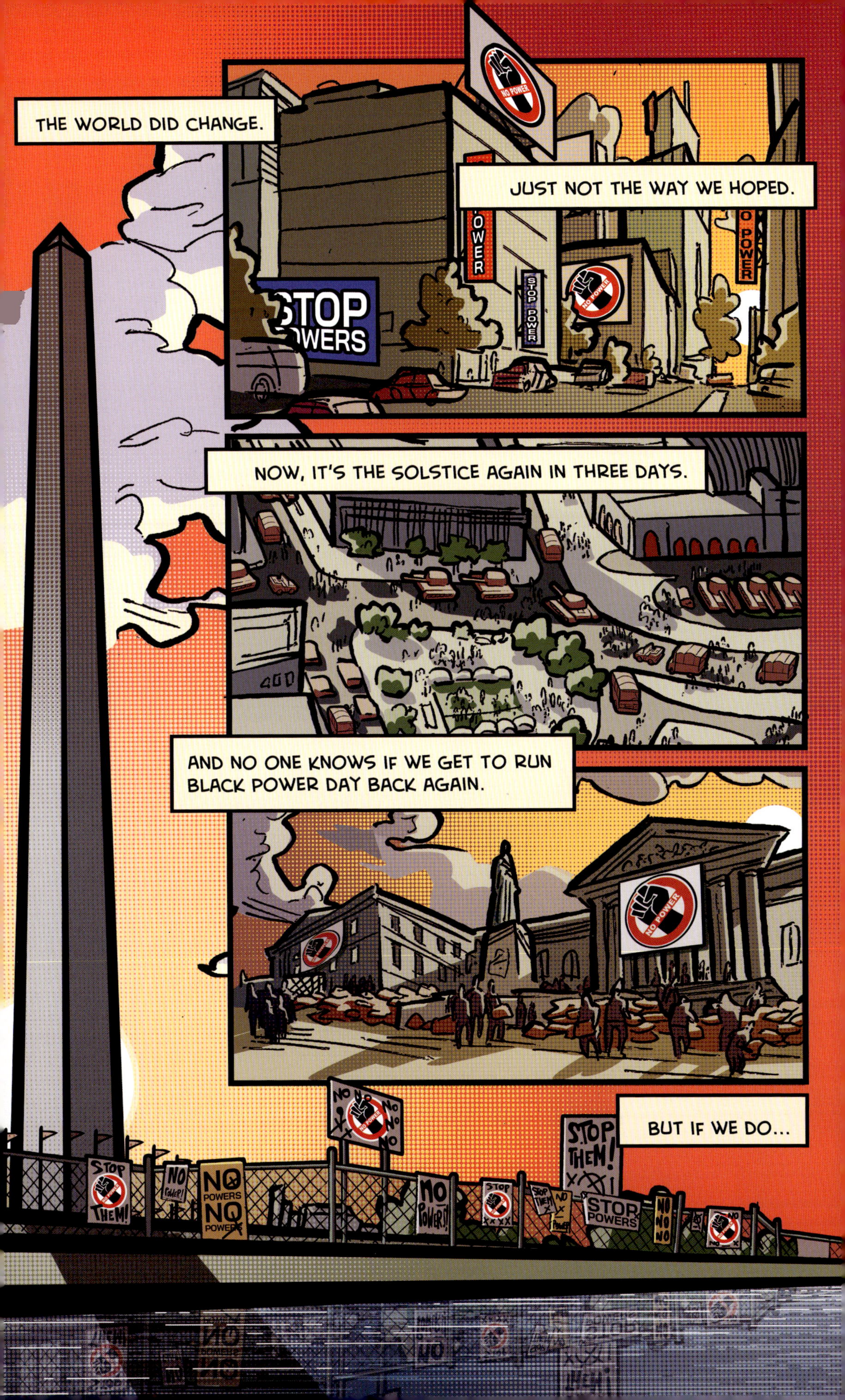
THE WORLD DID CHANGE.
JUST NOT THE WAY WE HOPED.
NO POWER
STOP POWERS
POWER
STOP POWER
NOW, IT'S THE SOLSTICE AGAIN IN THREE DAYS.
AND NO ONE KNOWS IF WE GET TO RUN BLACK POWER DAY BACK AGAIN.
BUT IF WE DO...
STOP THEM!
NO POWERS
NO POWERS!
STOP POWERS

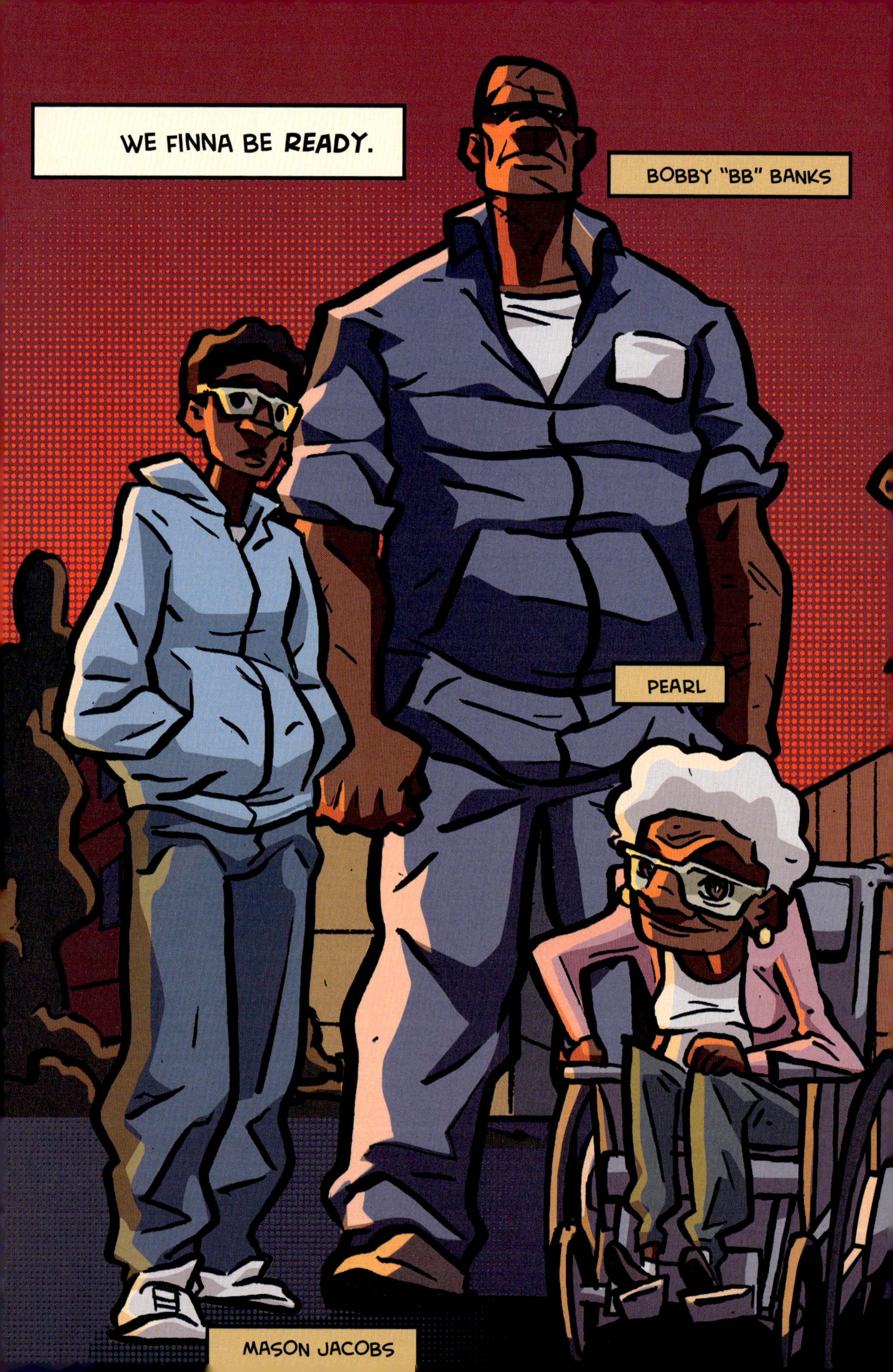
WE FINNA BE READY.
BOBBY "BB" BANKS
PEARL
MASON JACOBS

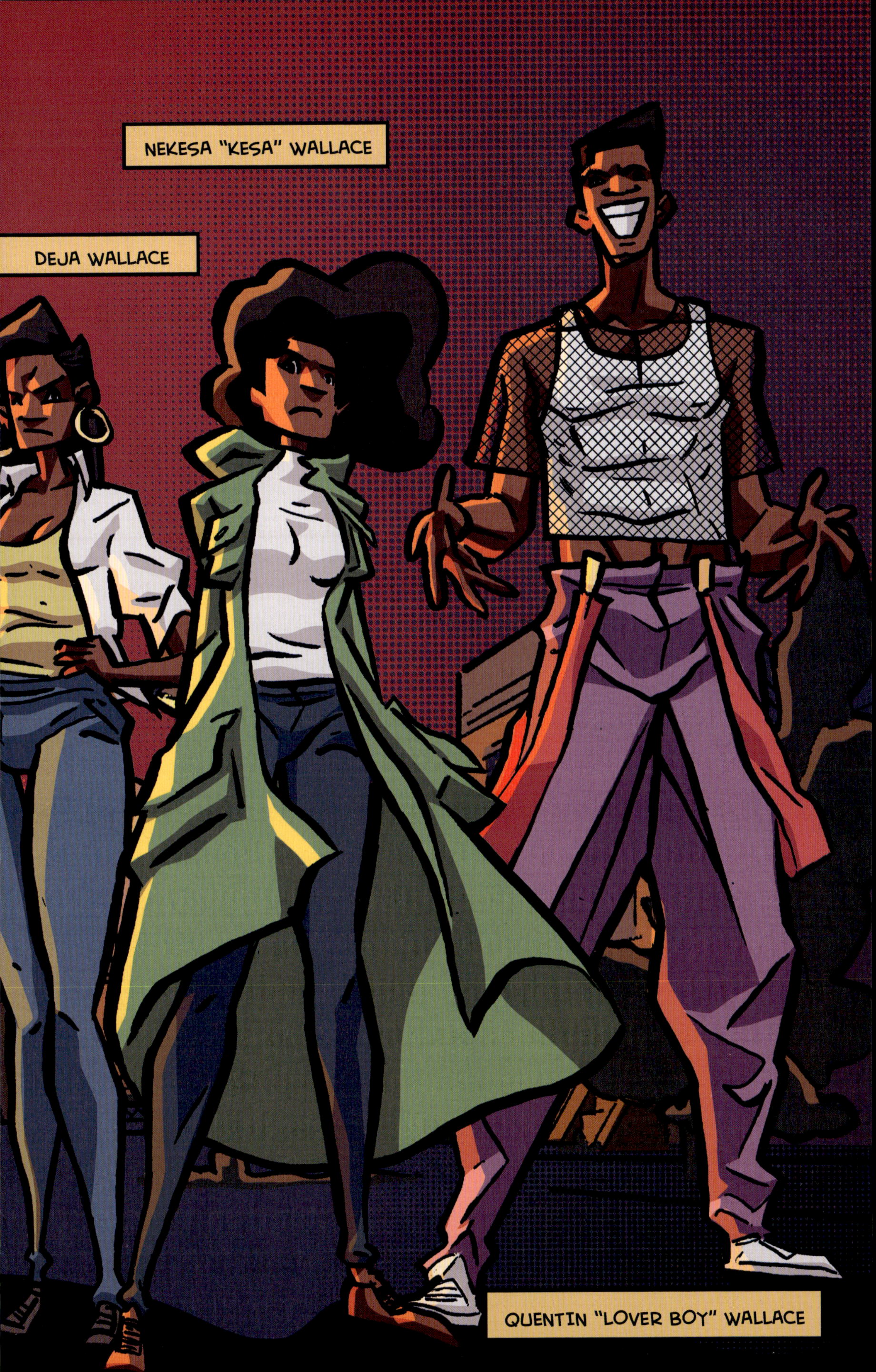
NEKESA "KESA" WALLACE
DEJA WALLACE
QUENTIN "LOVER BOY" WALLACE

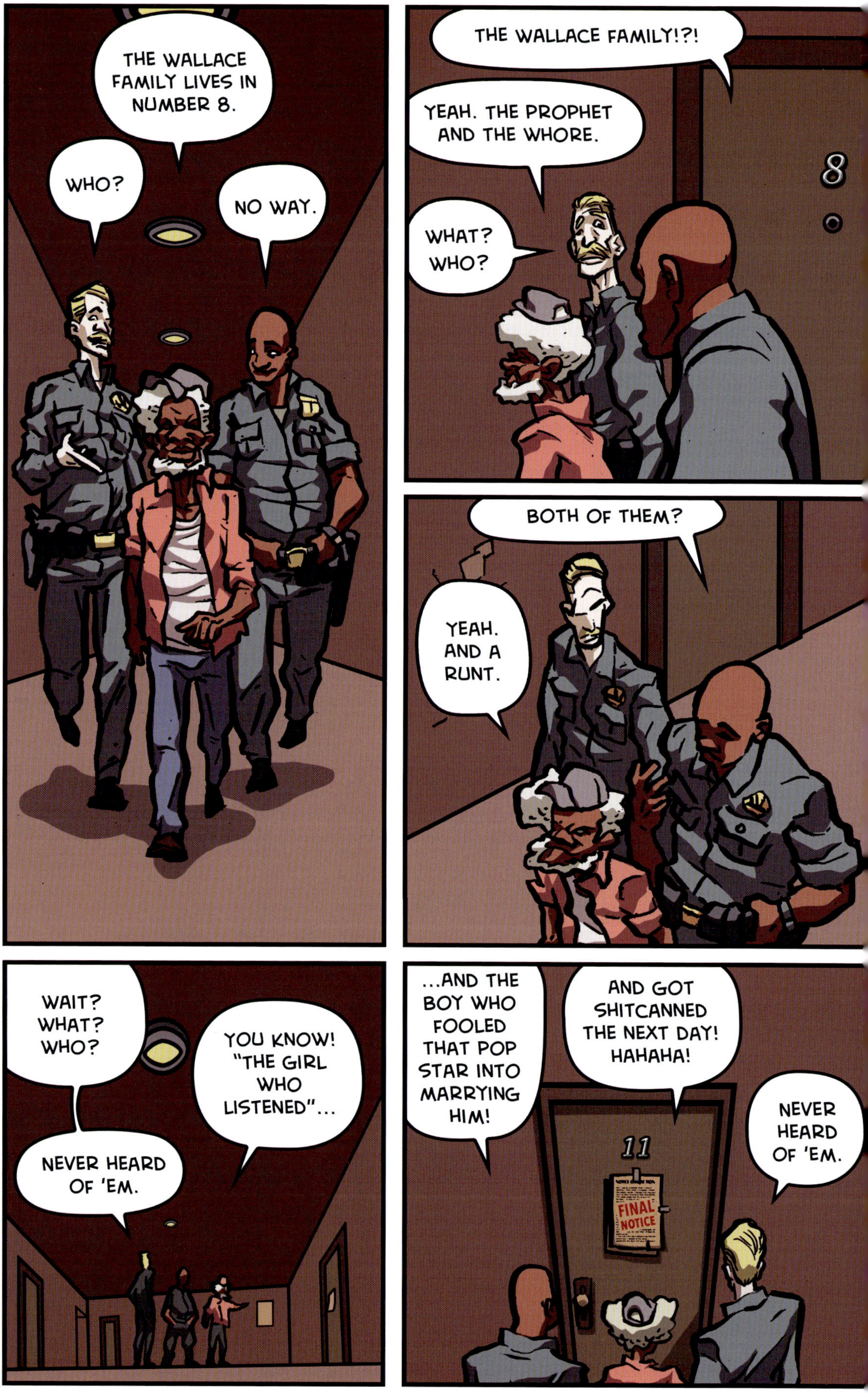
THE WALLACE FAMILY LIVES IN NUMBER 8.
WHO?
NO WAY.
THE WALLACE FAMILY!?!
YEAH. THE PROPHET AND THE WHORE.
8
WHAT? WHO?
BOTH OF THEM?
YEAH. AND A RUNT.
WAIT? WHAT? WHO?
YOU KNOW! "THE GIRL WHO LISTENED"...
NEVER HEARD OF 'EM.
...AND THE BOY WHO FOOLED THAT POP STAR INTO MARRYING HIM!
AND GOT SHITCANNED THE NEXT DAY! HAHAHA!
11
FINAL NOTICE
NEVER HEARD OF 'EM.

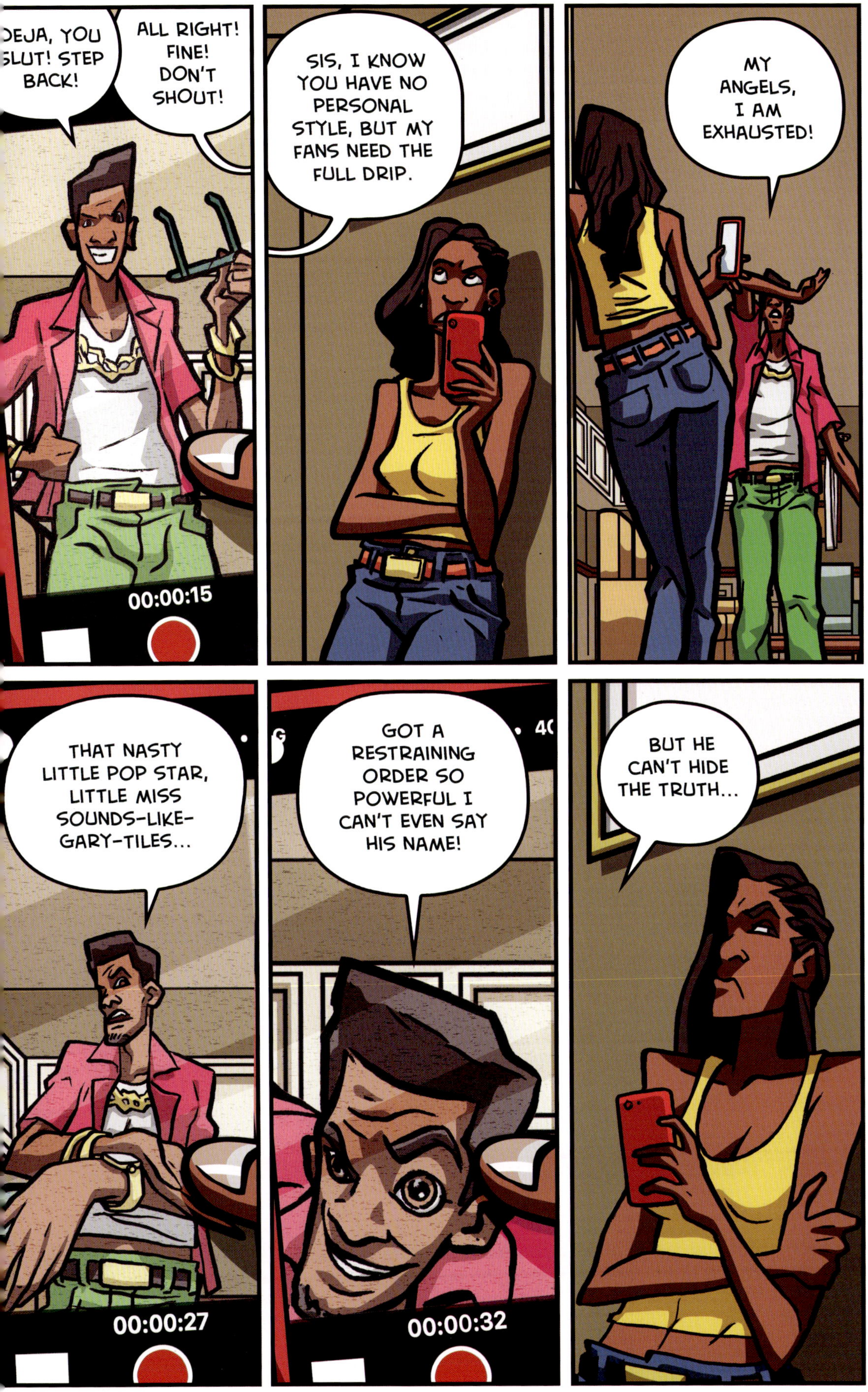
DEJA, YOU SLUT! STEP BACK!
ALL RIGHT! FINE! DON'T SHOUT!
00:00:15
SIS, I KNOW YOU HAVE NO PERSONAL STYLE, BUT MY FANS NEED THE FULL DRIP.
MY ANGELS, I AM EXHAUSTED!
THAT NASTY LITTLE POP STAR, LITTLE MISS SOUNDS-LIKE-GARY-TILES...
00:00:27
GOT A RESTRAINING ORDER SO POWERFUL I CAN'T EVEN SAY HIS NAME!
00:00:32
BUT HE CAN'T HIDE THE TRUTH...

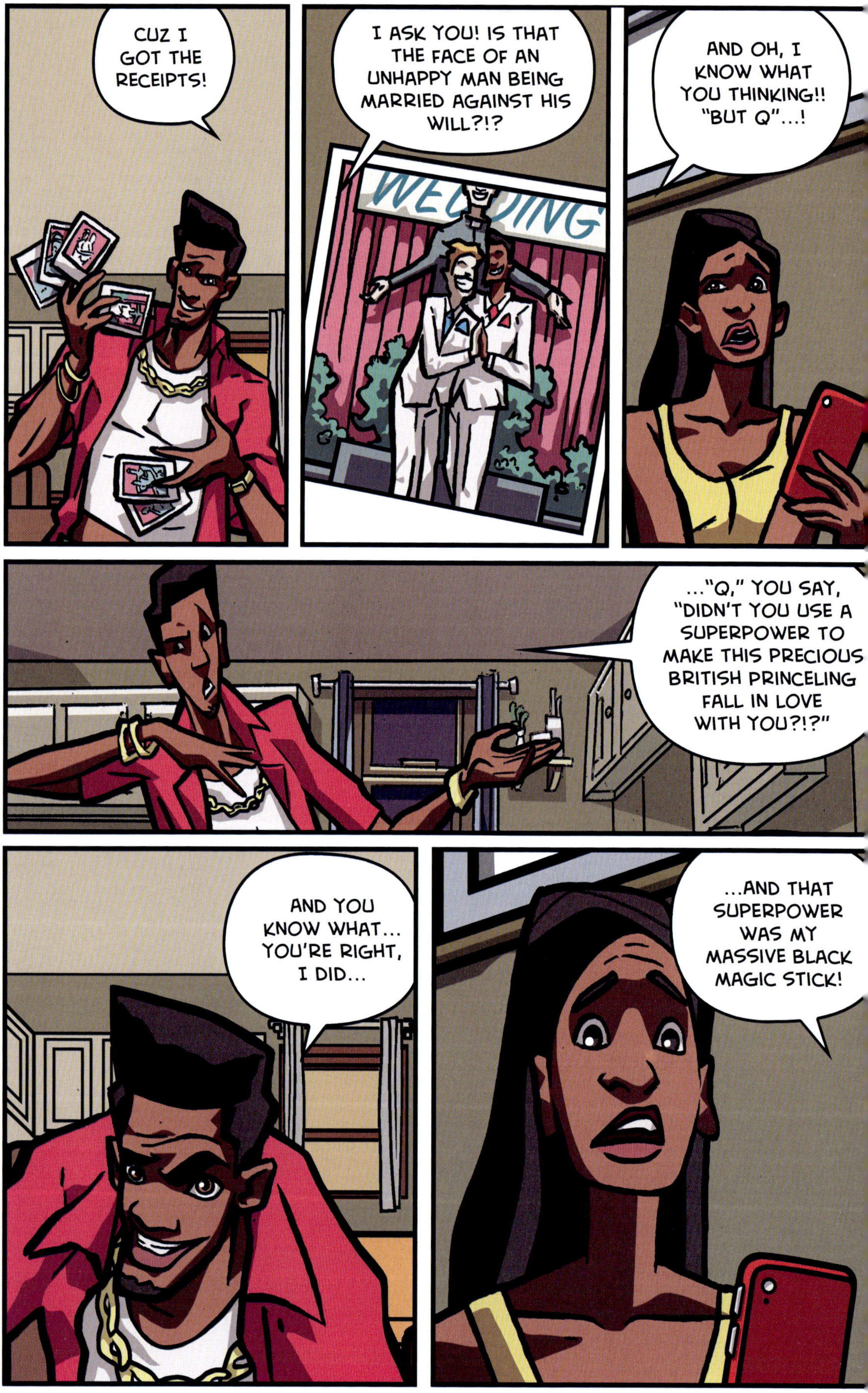
CUZ I GOT THE RECEIPTS!
I ASK YOU! IS THAT THE FACE OF AN UNHAPPY MAN BEING MARRIED AGAINST HIS WILL?!?
WEDDING
AND OH, I KNOW WHAT YOU THINKING!! "BUT Q"...!
..."Q," YOU SAY, "DIDN'T YOU USE A SUPERPOWER TO MAKE THIS PRECIOUS BRITISH PRINCELING FALL IN LOVE WITH YOU?!?"
AND YOU KNOW WHAT... YOU'RE RIGHT, I DID...
...AND THAT SUPERPOWER WAS MY MASSIVE BLACK MAGIC STICK!

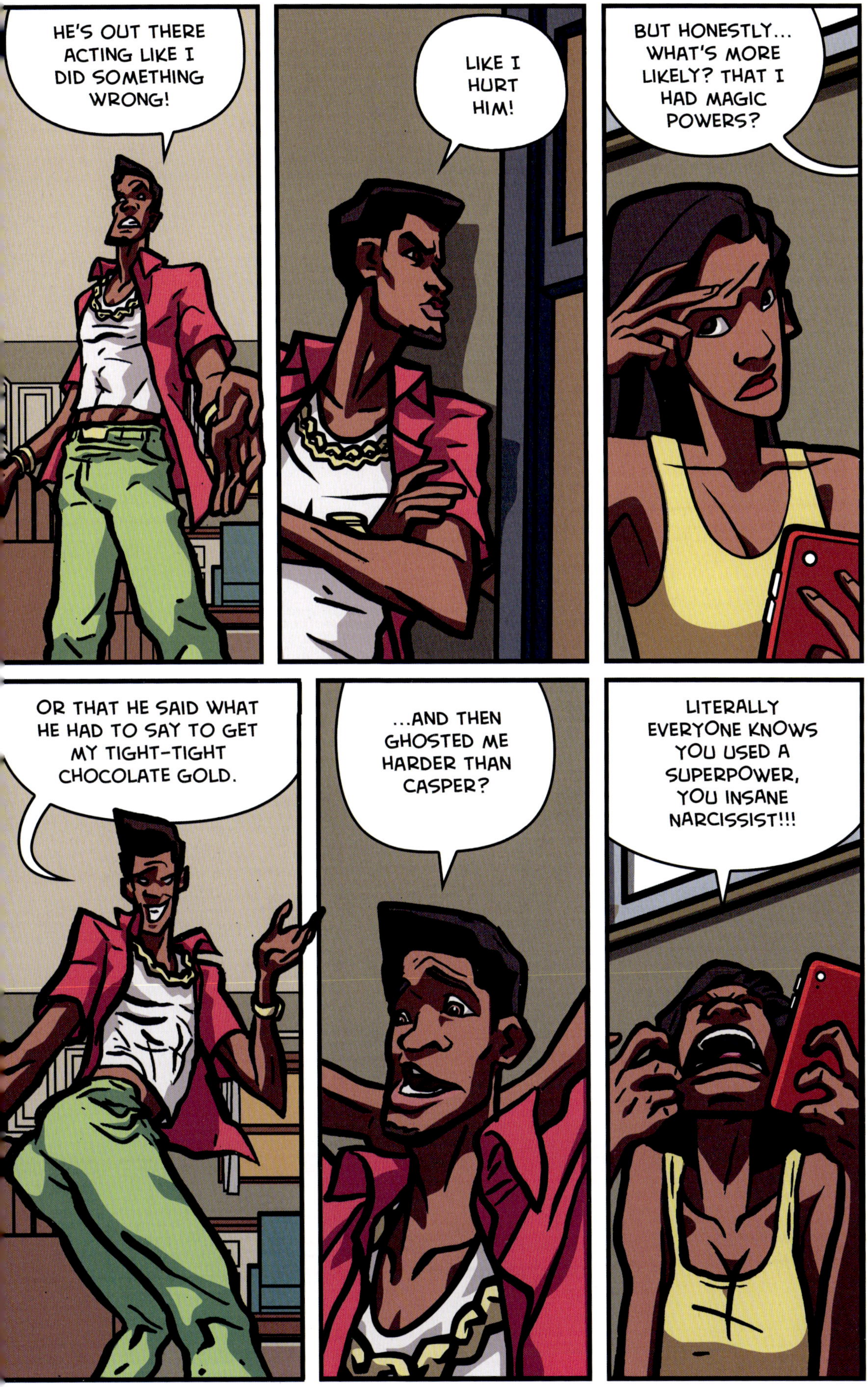
HE'S OUT THERE ACTING LIKE I DID SOMETHING WRONG!
LIKE I HURT HIM!
BUT HONESTLY... WHAT'S MORE LIKELY? THAT I HAD MAGIC POWERS?
OR THAT HE SAID WHAT HE HAD TO SAY TO GET MY TIGHT-TIGHT CHOCOLATE GOLD.
...AND THEN GHOSTED ME HARDER THAN CASPER?
LITERALLY EVERYONE KNOWS YOU USED A SUPERPOWER, YOU INSANE NARCISSIST!!!

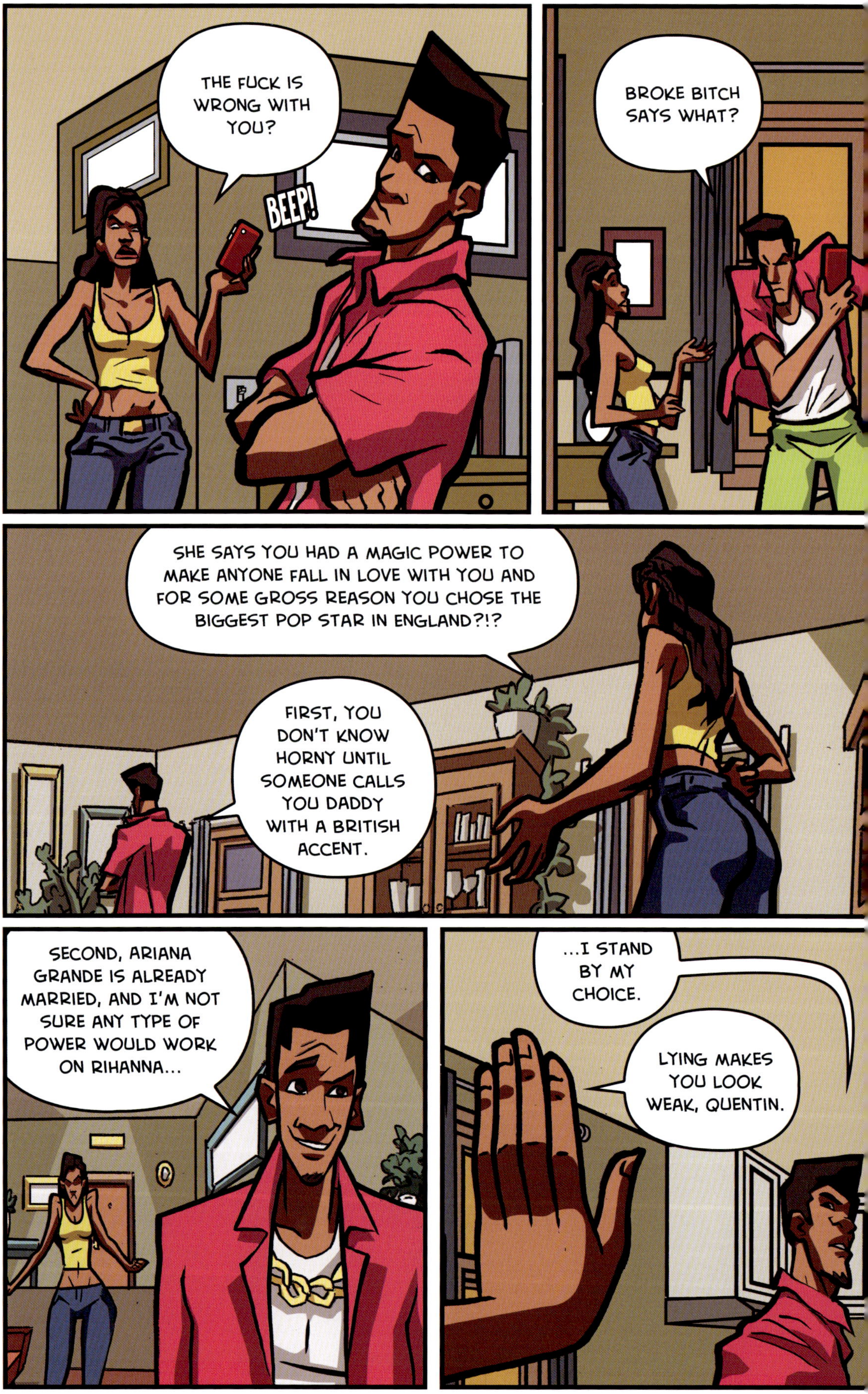
THE FUCK IS WRONG WITH YOU?
BEEP!
BROKE BITCH SAYS WHAT?
SHE SAYS YOU HAD A MAGIC POWER TO MAKE ANYONE FALL IN LOVE WITH YOU AND FOR SOME GROSS REASON YOU CHOSE THE BIGGEST POP STAR IN ENGLAND?!?
FIRST, YOU DON'T KNOW HORNY UNTIL SOMEONE CALLS YOU DADDY WITH A BRITISH ACCENT.
SECOND, ARIANA GRANDE IS ALREADY MARRIED, AND I'M NOT SURE ANY TYPE OF POWER WOULD WORK ON RIHANNA...
...I STAND BY MY CHOICE.
LYING MAKES YOU LOOK WEAK, QUENTIN.

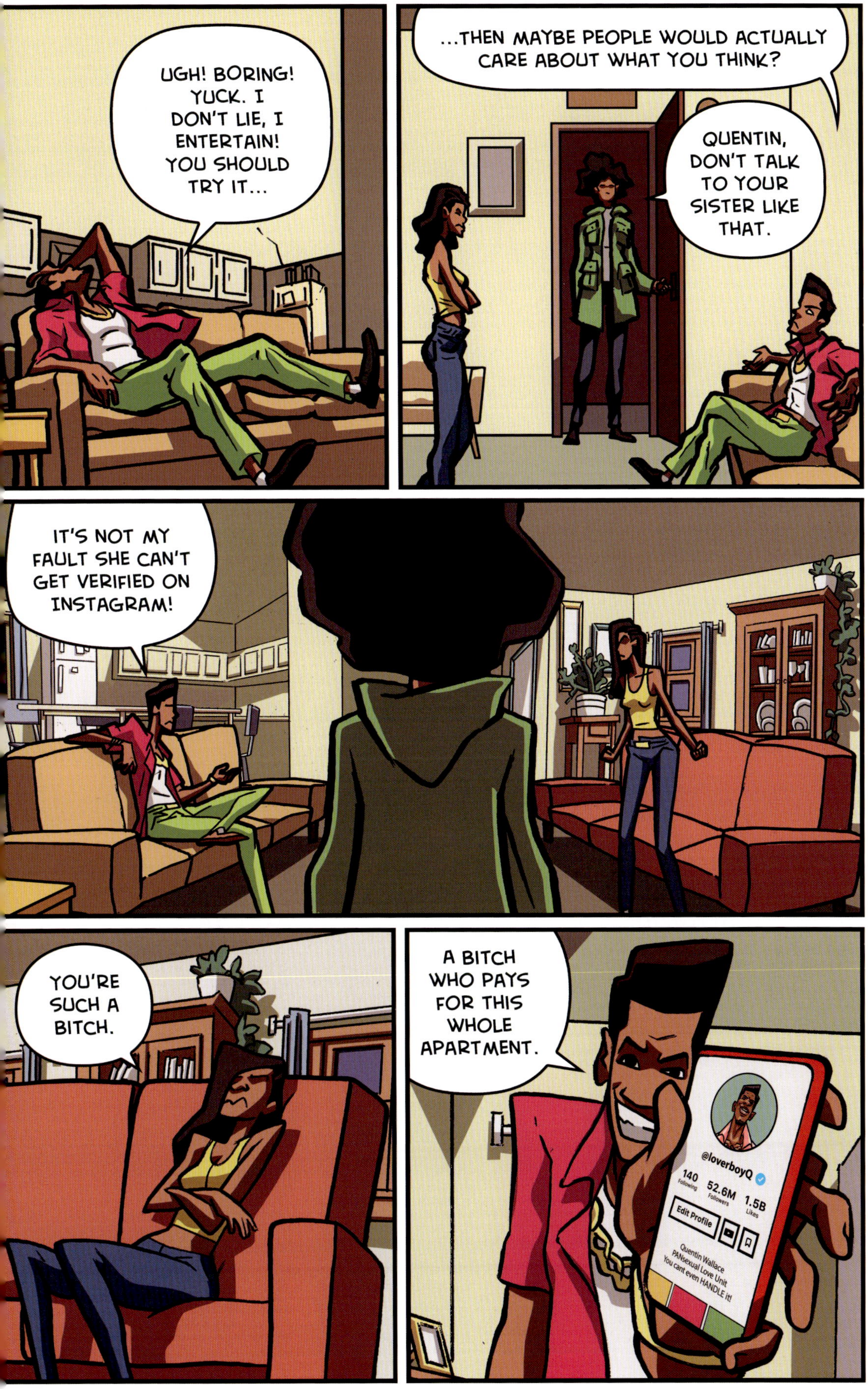
UGH! BORING! YUCK. I DON'T LIE, I ENTERTAIN! YOU SHOULD TRY IT...
...THEN MAYBE PEOPLE WOULD ACTUALLY CARE ABOUT WHAT YOU THINK?
QUENTIN, DON'T TALK TO YOUR SISTER LIKE THAT.
IT'S NOT MY FAULT SHE CAN'T GET VERIFIED ON INSTAGRAM!
YOU'RE SUCH A BITCH.
A BITCH WHO PAYS FOR THIS WHOLE APARTMENT.
@loverboyQ
140 Following
52.6M Followers
1.5B Likes
Edit Profile
Quentin Wallace
PANsexual Love Unit
You cant even HANDLE it!

BOTH OF YOU, SHUT UP AND GET TO CLEANING. NOW!
WE START TOMORROW, QUENTIN.
IS EVERYONE COMING OVER?
BUT THEN WHY IS SHE HERE?
I THOUGHT ONLY NIGGAS WITH SUPERPOWERS COULD PLAY?
THIS YEAR SHE'LL GET POWERS.
WHAT IF WE DON'T GET POWERS THIS YEAR?
WE WILL.
THEN WE'LL STILL HAVE A TIDY FUCKING APARTMENT. NOW MOVE.
AARGHHHHHHHHHH!
GET YOUR FUCKING HANDS OFF ME!

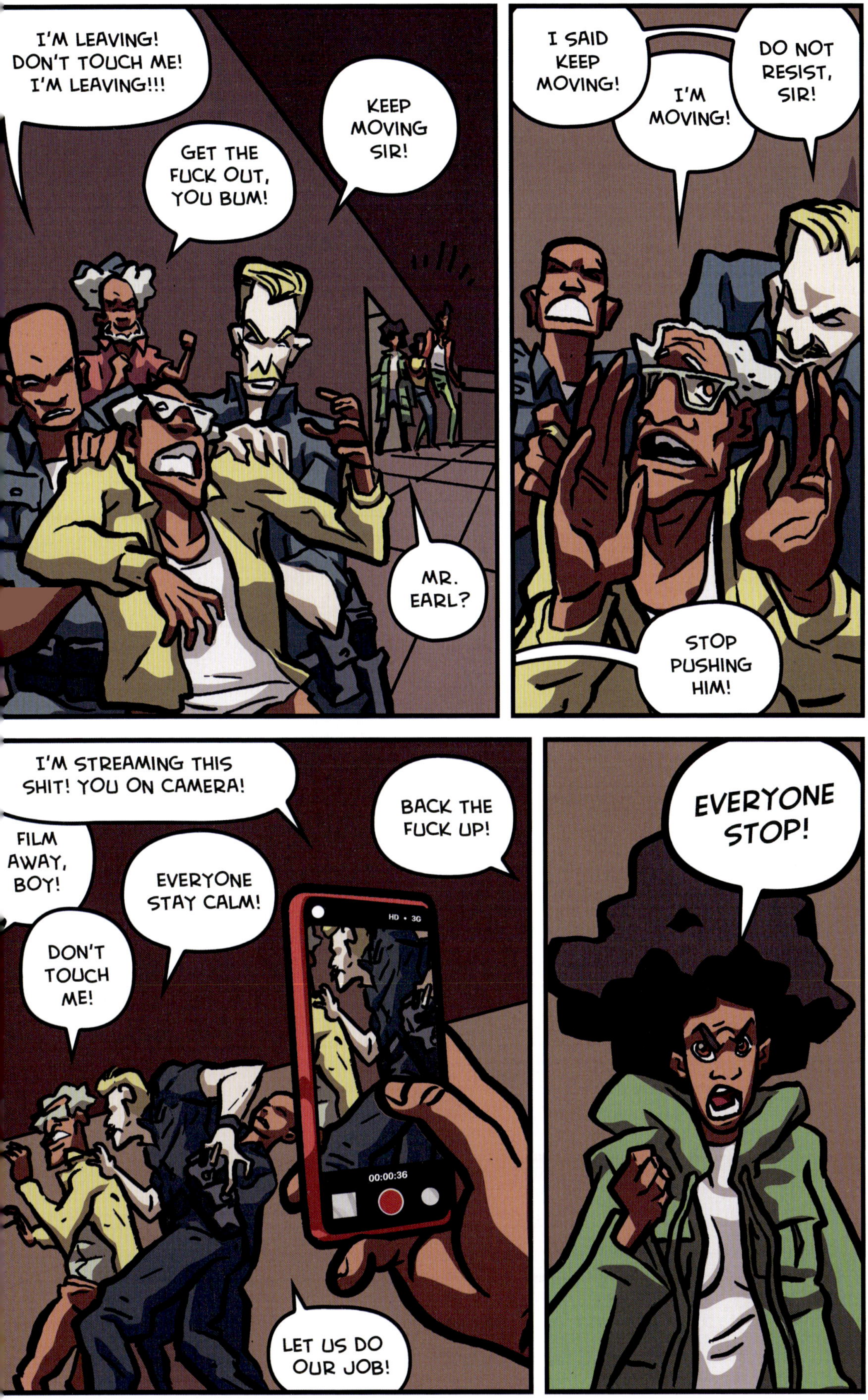
I'M LEAVING! DON'T TOUCH ME! I'M LEAVING!!!
GET THE FUCK OUT, YOU BUM!
KEEP MOVING SIR!
MR. EARL?
I SAID KEEP MOVING!
I'M MOVING!
DO NOT RESIST, SIR!
STOP PUSHING HIM!
I'M STREAMING THIS SHIT! YOU ON CAMERA!
FILM AWAY, BOY!
EVERYONE STAY CALM!
BACK THE FUCK UP!
DON'T TOUCH ME!
HD • 3G
00:00:36
LET US DO OUR JOB!
EVERYONE STOP!

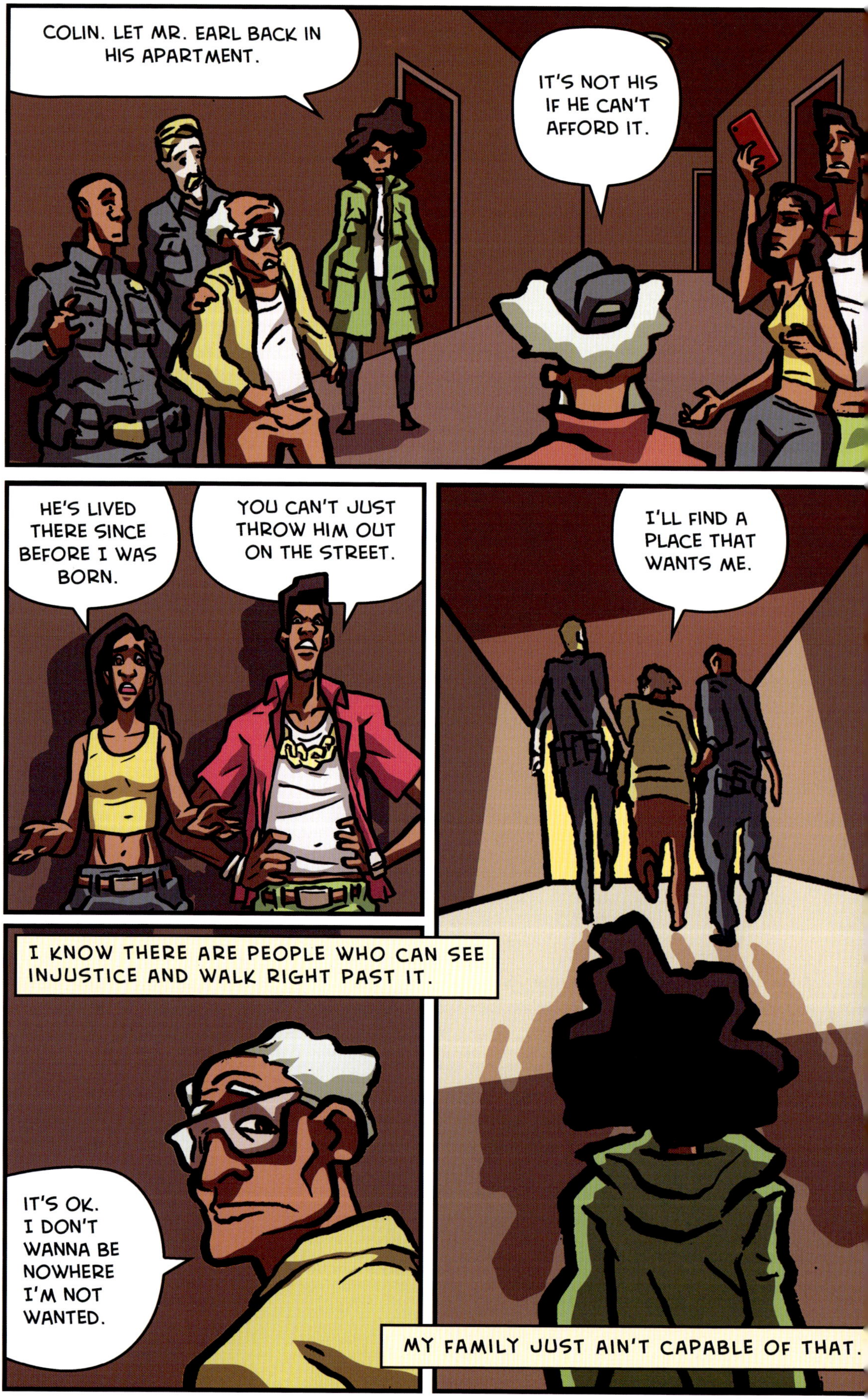
COLIN. LET MR. EARL BACK IN HIS APARTMENT.
IT'S NOT HIS IF HE CAN'T AFFORD IT.
HE'S LIVED THERE SINCE BEFORE I WAS BORN.
YOU CAN'T JUST THROW HIM OUT ON THE STREET.
I KNOW THERE ARE PEOPLE WHO CAN SEE INJUSTICE AND WALK RIGHT PAST IT.
IT'S OK. I DON'T WANNA BE NOWHERE I'M NOT WANTED.
I'LL FIND A PLACE THAT WANTS ME.
MY FAMILY JUST AIN'T CAPABLE OF THAT.

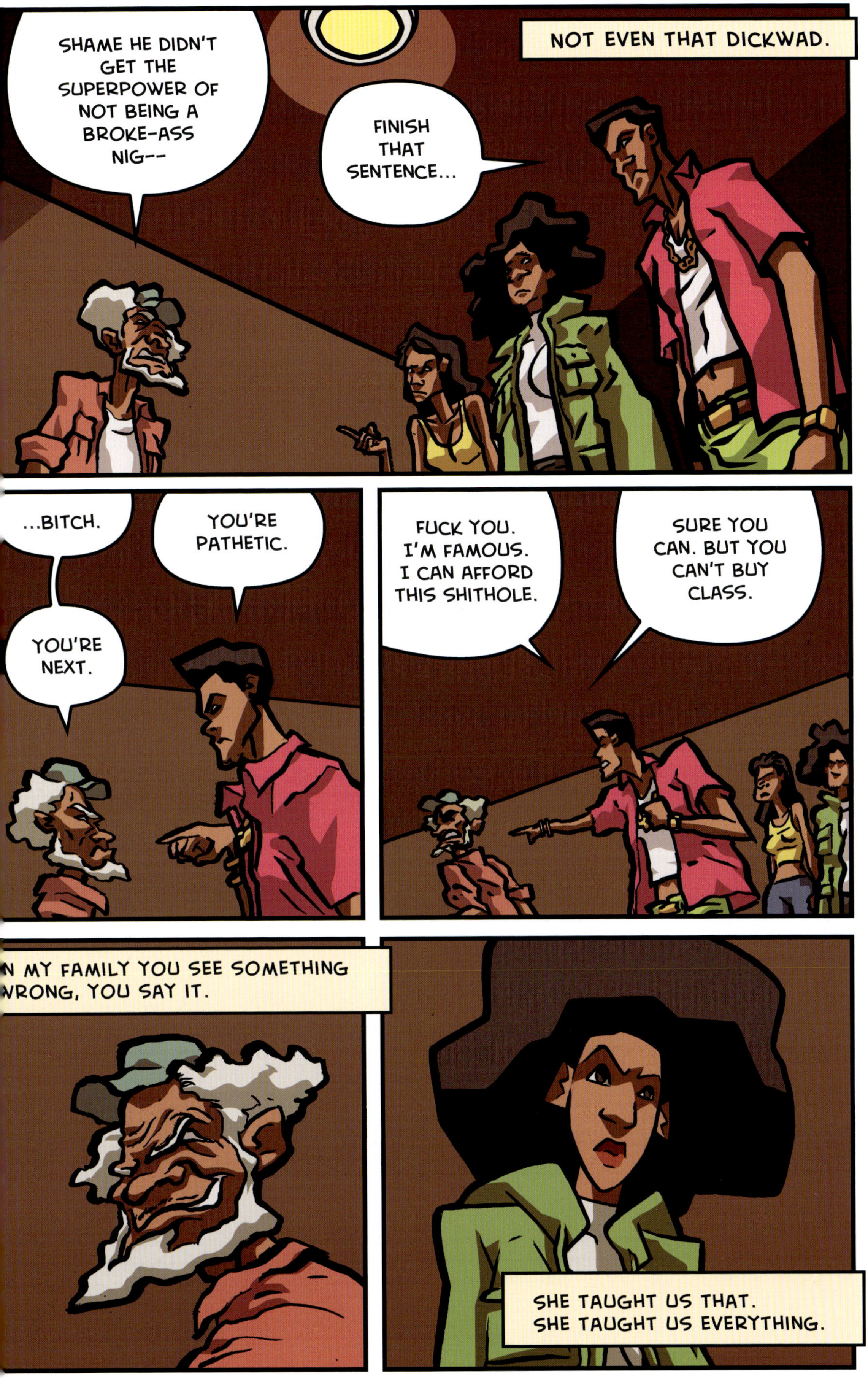
SHAME HE DIDN'T GET THE SUPERPOWER OF NOT BEING A BROKE-ASS NIG--
FINISH THAT SENTENCE...
NOT EVEN THAT DICKWAD.
...BITCH.
YOU'RE PATHETIC.
YOU'RE NEXT.
FUCK YOU. I'M FAMOUS. I CAN AFFORD THIS SHITHOLE.
SURE YOU CAN. BUT YOU CAN'T BUY CLASS.
N MY FAMILY YOU SEE SOMETHING
VRONG, YOU SAY IT.
SHE TAUGHT US THAT.
SHE TAUGHT US EVERYTHING.

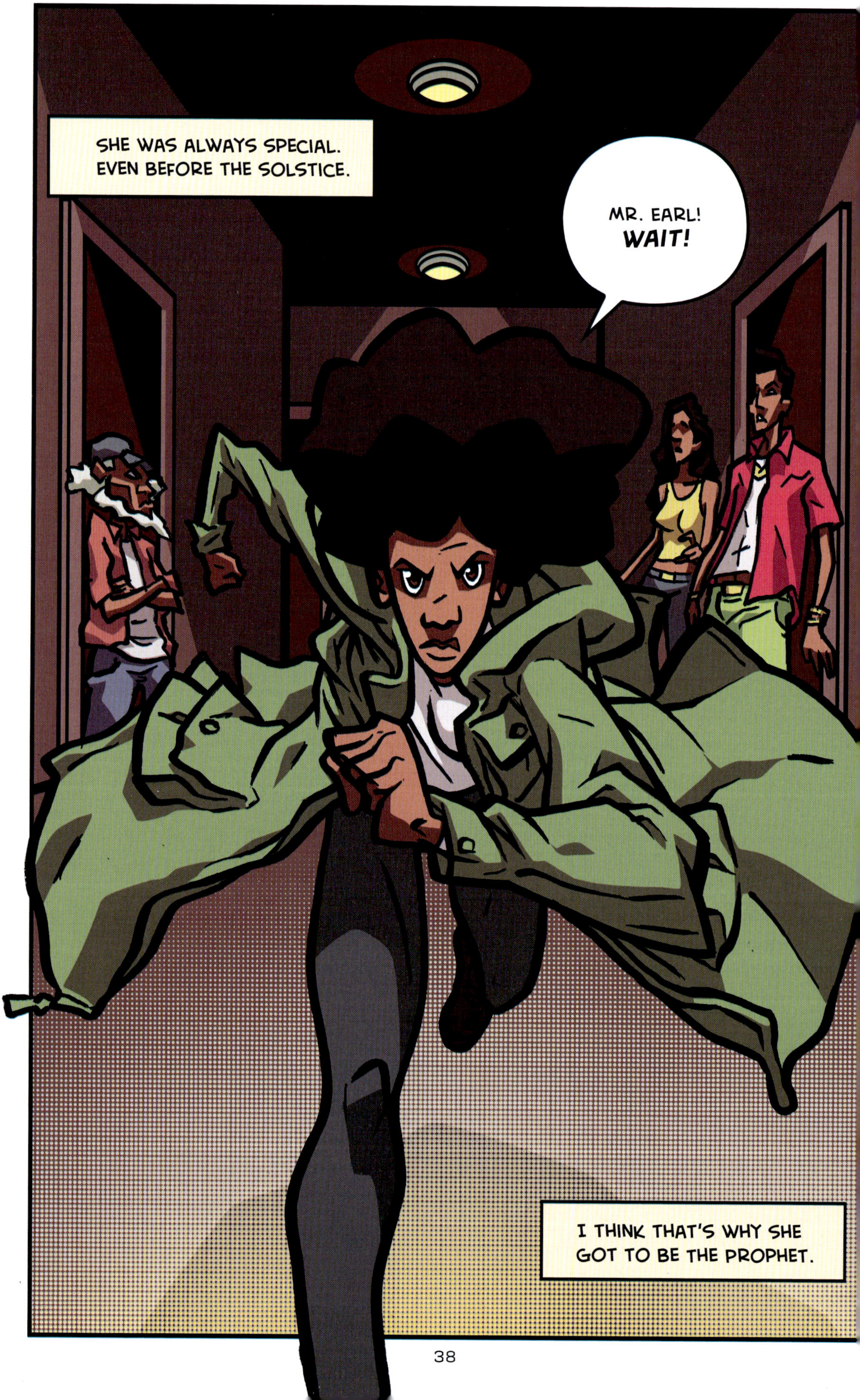
SHE WAS ALWAYS SPECIAL. EVEN BEFORE THE SOLSTICE.
MR. EARL! **WAIT!**
I THINK THAT'S WHY SHE GOT TO BE THE PROPHET.

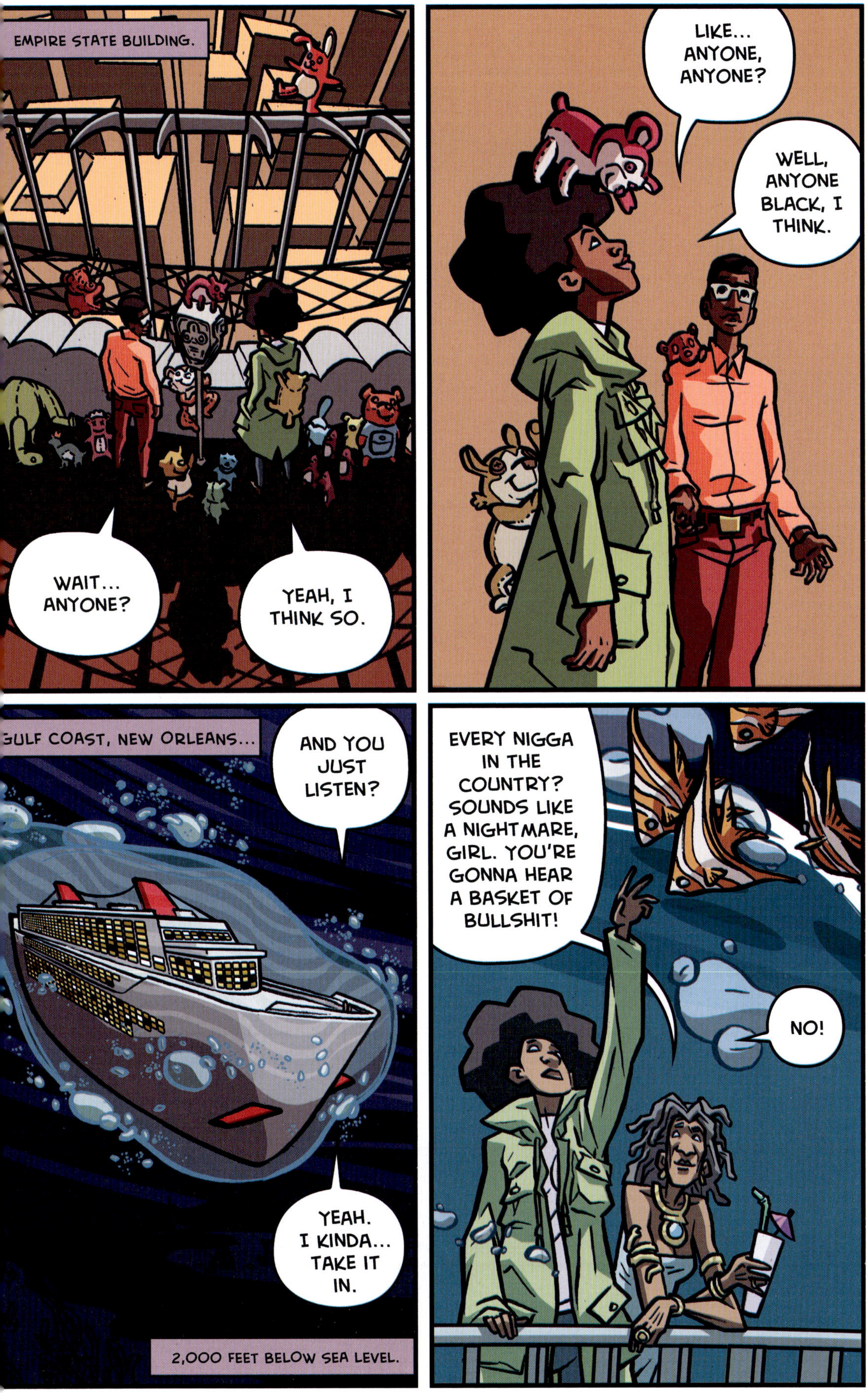
EMPIRE STATE BUILDING.
WAIT... ANYONE?
YEAH, I THINK SO.
LIKE... ANYONE, ANYONE?
WELL, ANYONE BLACK, I THINK.
GULF COAST, NEW ORLEANS...
AND YOU JUST LISTEN?
YEAH. I KINDA... TAKE IT IN.
2,000 FEET BELOW SEA LEVEL.
EVERY NIGGA IN THE COUNTRY? SOUNDS LIKE A NIGHTMARE, GIRL. YOU'RE GONNA HEAR A BASKET OF BULLSHIT!
NO!

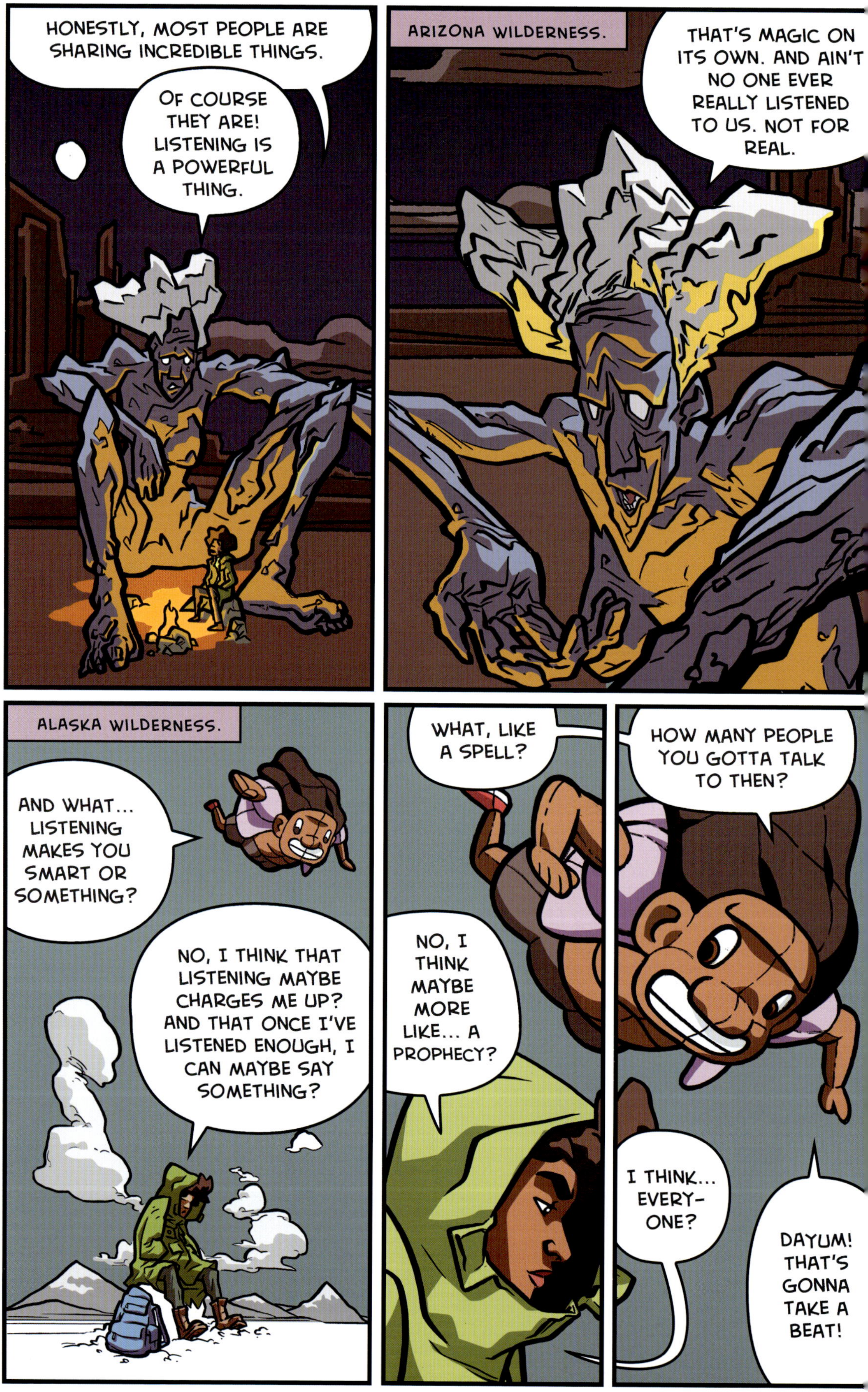
HONESTLY, MOST PEOPLE ARE SHARING INCREDIBLE THINGS.
OF COURSE THEY ARE! LISTENING IS A POWERFUL THING.
ARIZONA WILDERNESS.
THAT'S MAGIC ON ITS OWN. AND AIN'T NO ONE EVER REALLY LISTENED TO US. NOT FOR REAL.
ALASKA WILDERNESS.
AND WHAT... LISTENING MAKES YOU SMART OR SOMETHING?
NO, I THINK THAT LISTENING MAYBE CHARGES ME UP? AND THAT ONCE I'VE LISTENED ENOUGH, I CAN MAYBE SAY SOMETHING?
WHAT, LIKE A SPELL?
NO, I THINK MAYBE MORE LIKE... A PROPHECY?
HOW MANY PEOPLE YOU GOTTA TALK TO THEN?
I THINK... EVERY-ONE?
DAYUM! THAT'S GONNA TAKE A BEAT!

I DON'T THINK SO.
I'M NOT TOTALLY SURE, BUT I DON'T THINK I'M JUST TALKING TO YOU RIGHT NOW.
I THINK, MAYBE, I'M TALKING TO A LOT OF PEOPLE RIGHT NOW.

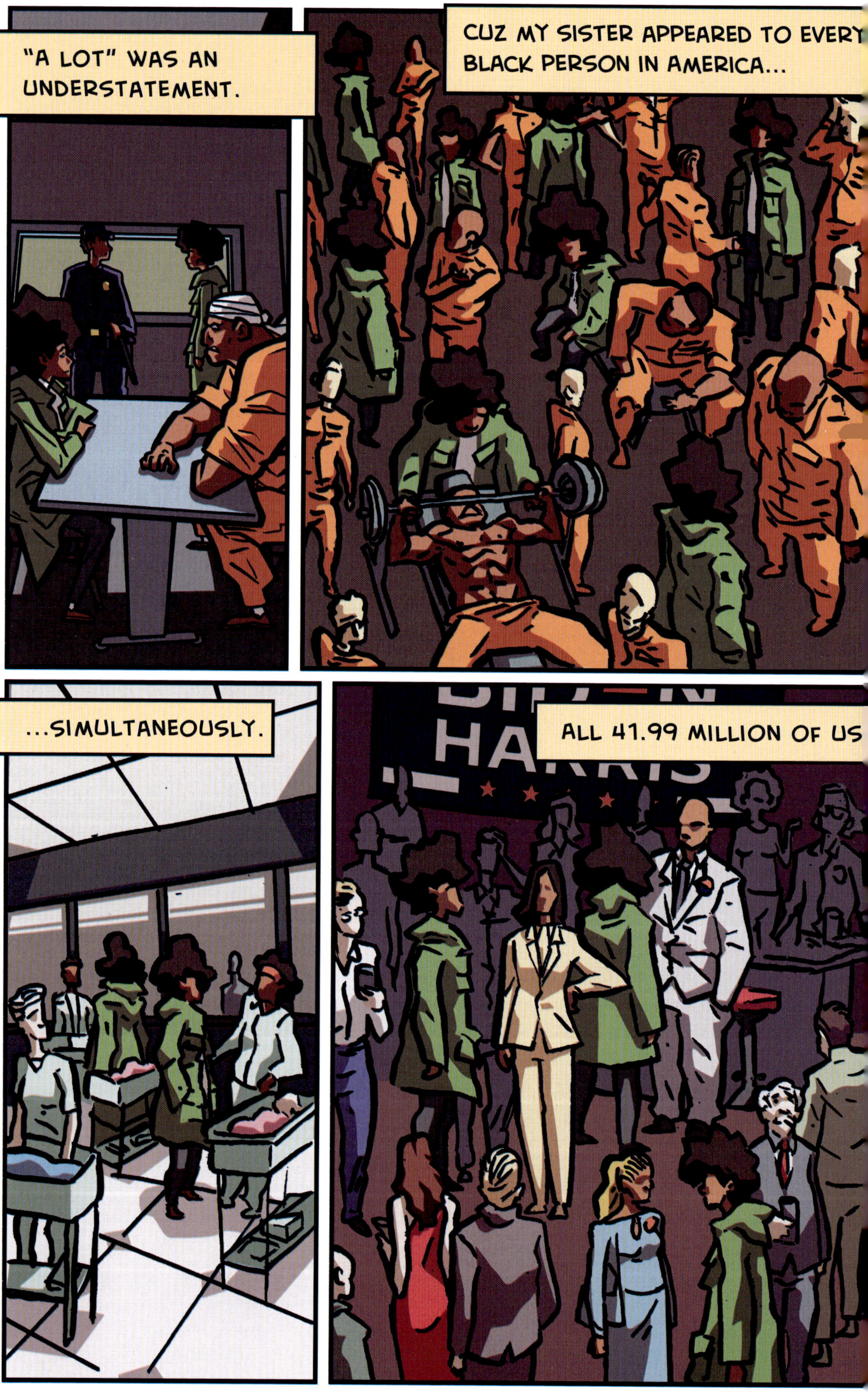
"A LOT" WAS AN UNDERSTATEMENT.
CUZ MY SISTER APPEARED TO EVERY BLACK PERSON IN AMERICA...
...SIMULTANEOUSLY.
ALL 41.99 MILLION OF US

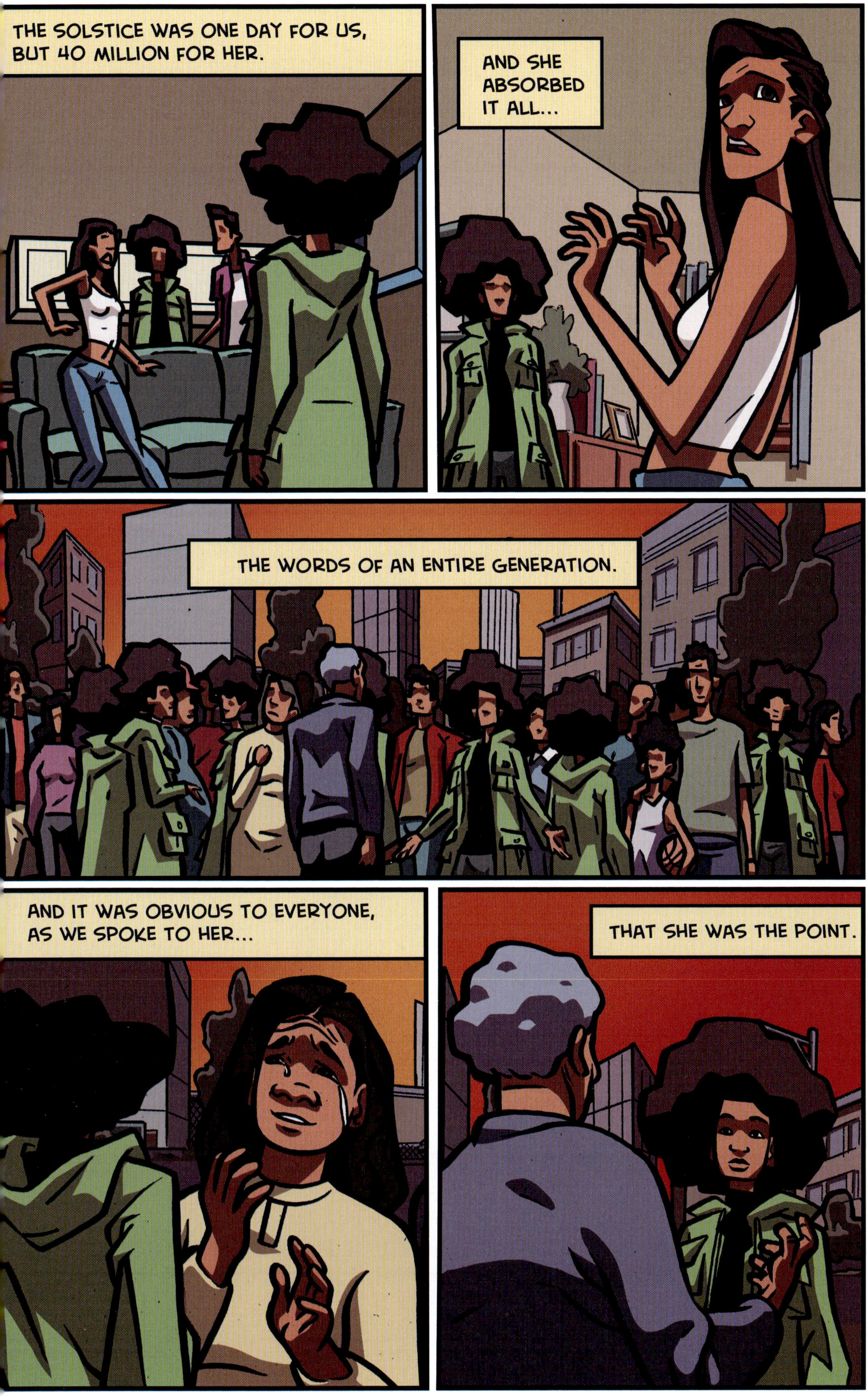
THE SOLSTICE WAS ONE DAY FOR US, BUT 40 MILLION FOR HER.
AND SHE ABSORBED IT ALL...
THE WORDS OF AN ENTIRE GENERATION.
AND IT WAS OBVIOUS TO EVERYONE, AS WE SPOKE TO HER...
THAT SHE WAS THE POINT.

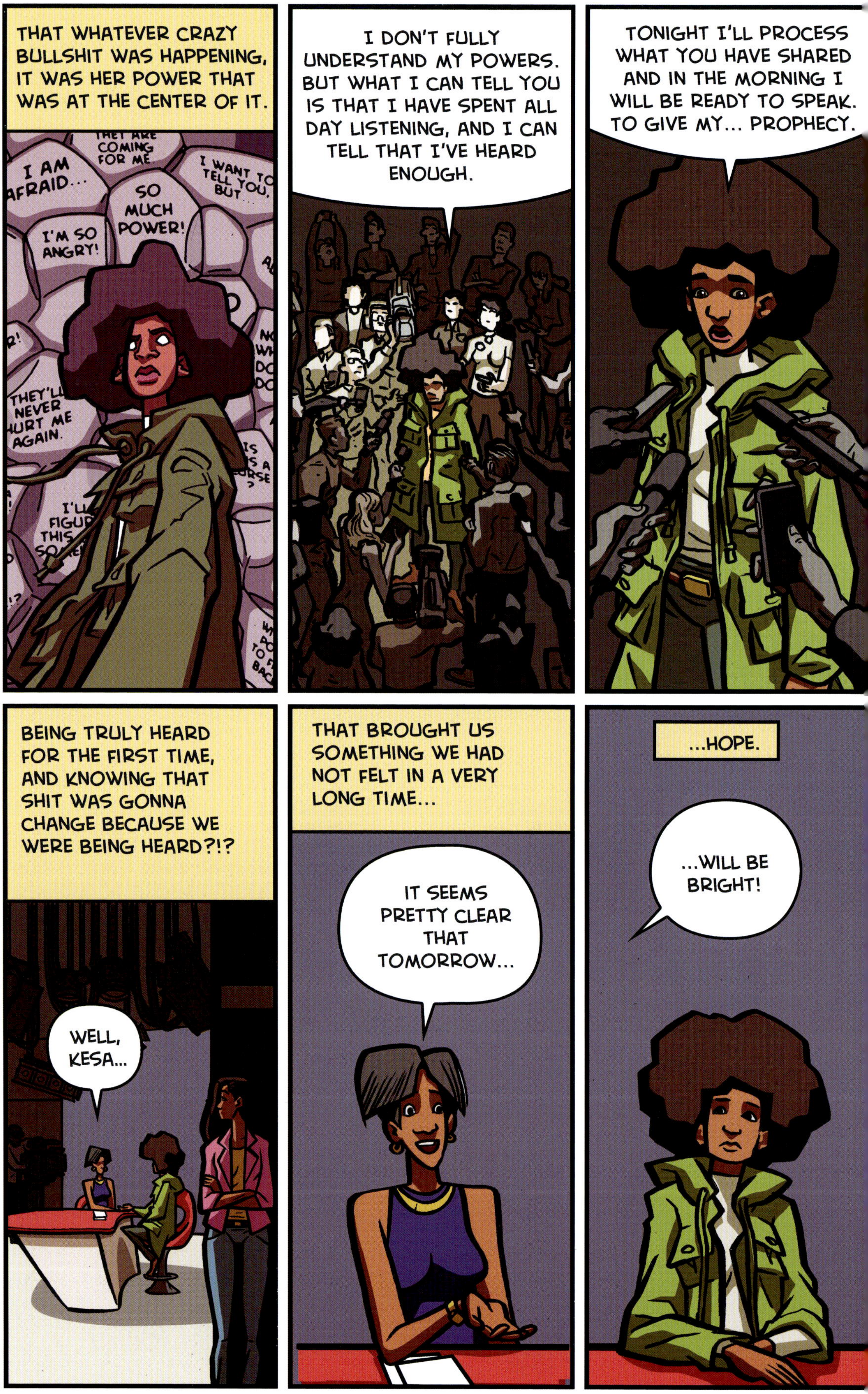
THAT WHATEVER CRAZY BULLSHIT WAS HAPPENING, IT WAS HER POWER THAT WAS AT THE CENTER OF IT.
COMING FOR ME.
SO MUCH POWER!
I'M SO ANGRY!
I DON'T FULLY UNDERSTAND MY POWERS. BUT WHAT I CAN TELL YOU IS THAT I HAVE SPENT ALL DAY LISTENING, AND I CAN TELL THAT I'VE HEARD ENOUGH.
TONIGHT I'LL PROCESS WHAT YOU HAVE SHARED AND IN THE MORNING I WILL BE READY TO SPEAK. TO GIVE MY... PROPHECY.
BEING TRULY HEARD FOR THE FIRST TIME, AND KNOWING THAT SHIT WAS GONNA CHANGE BECAUSE WE WERE BEING HEARD?!?
WELL, KESA...
THAT BROUGHT US SOMETHING WE HAD NOT FELT IN A VERY LONG TIME...
IT SEEMS PRETTY CLEAR THAT TOMORROW...
...HOPE.
...WILL BE BRIGHT!

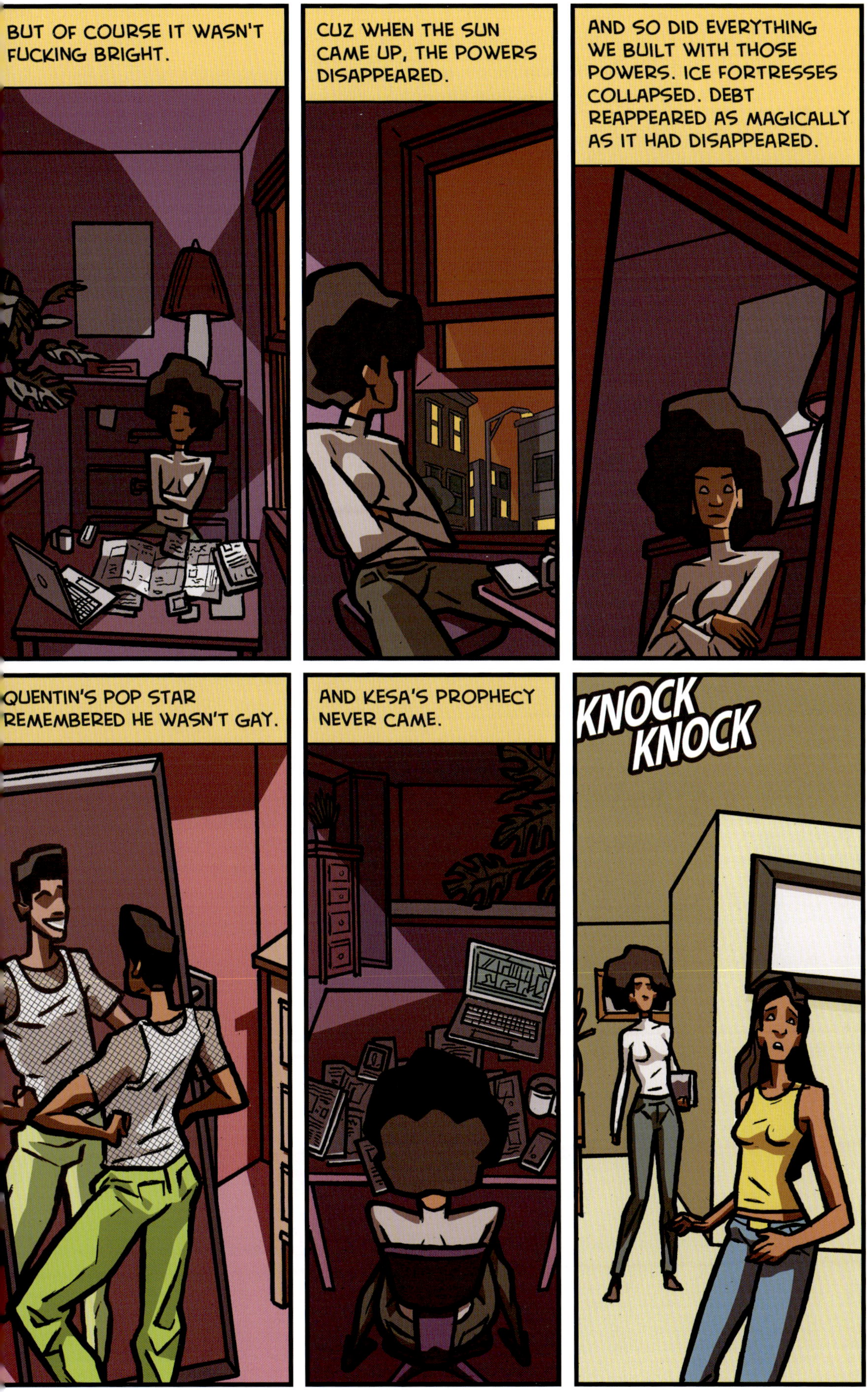
BUT OF COURSE IT WASN'T FUCKING BRIGHT.
CUZ WHEN THE SUN CAME UP, THE POWERS DISAPPEARED.
AND SO DID EVERYTHING WE BUILT WITH THOSE POWERS. ICE FORTRESSES COLLAPSED. DEBT REAPPEARED AS MAGICALLY AS IT HAD DISAPPEARED.
QUENTIN'S POP STAR REMEMBERED HE WASN'T GAY.
AND KESA'S PROPHECY NEVER CAME.
KNOCK KNOCK

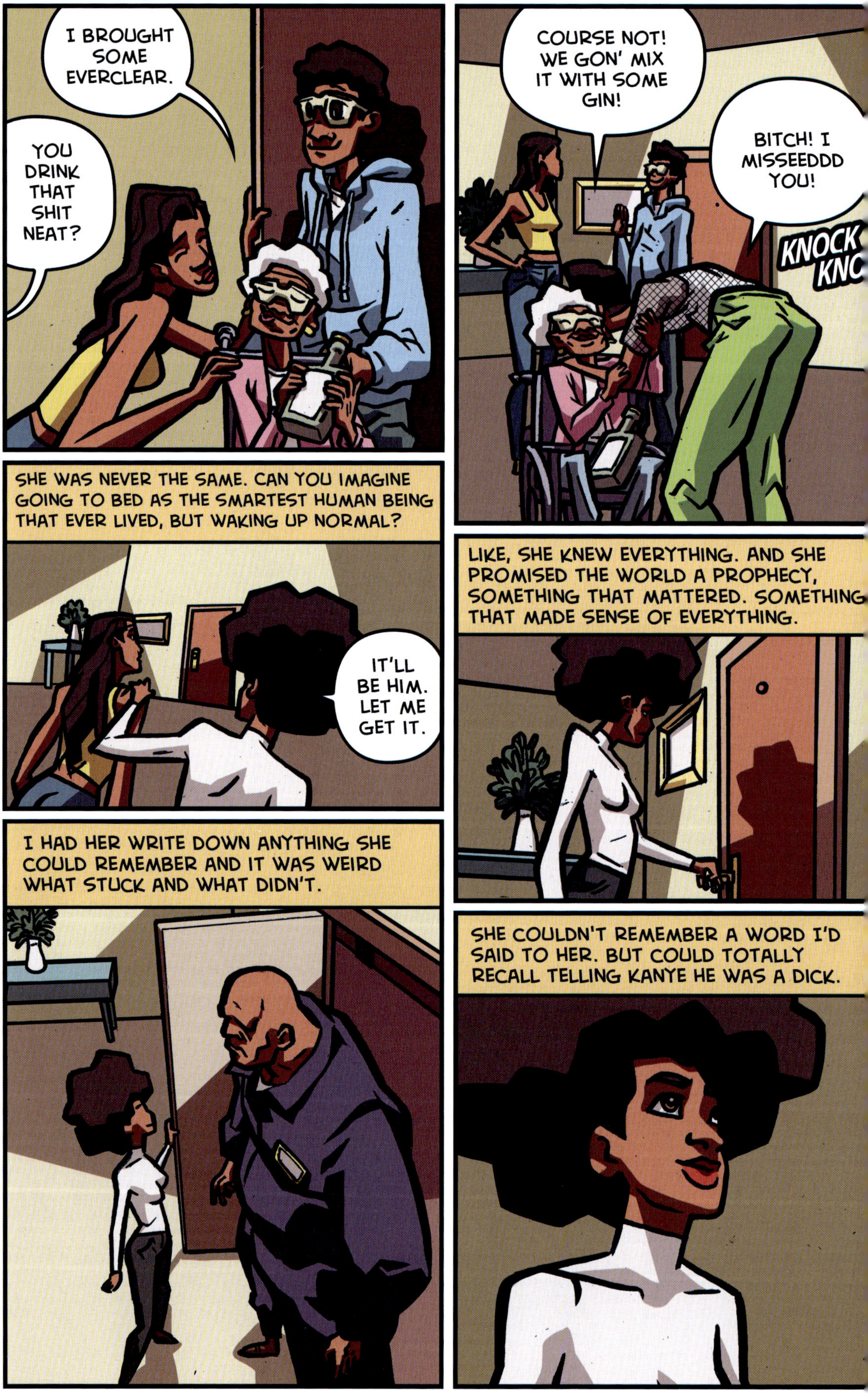
I BROUGHT SOME EVERCLEAR.
YOU DRINK THAT SHIT NEAT?
COURSE NOT! WE GON' MIX IT WITH SOME GIN!
BITCH! I MISSEEDDD YOU!
KNOCK KNC
SHE WAS NEVER THE SAME. CAN YOU IMAGINE GOING TO BED AS THE SMARTEST HUMAN BEING THAT EVER LIVED, BUT WAKING UP NORMAL?
IT'LL BE HIM. LET ME GET IT.
LIKE, SHE KNEW EVERYTHING. AND SHE PROMISED THE WORLD A PROPHECY, SOMETHING THAT MATTERED. SOMETHING THAT MADE SENSE OF EVERYTHING.
I HAD HER WRITE DOWN ANYTHING SHE COULD REMEMBER AND IT WAS WEIRD WHAT STUCK AND WHAT DIDN'T.
SHE COULDN'T REMEMBER A WORD I'D SAID TO HER. BUT COULD TOTALLY RECALL TELLING KANYE HE WAS A DICK.

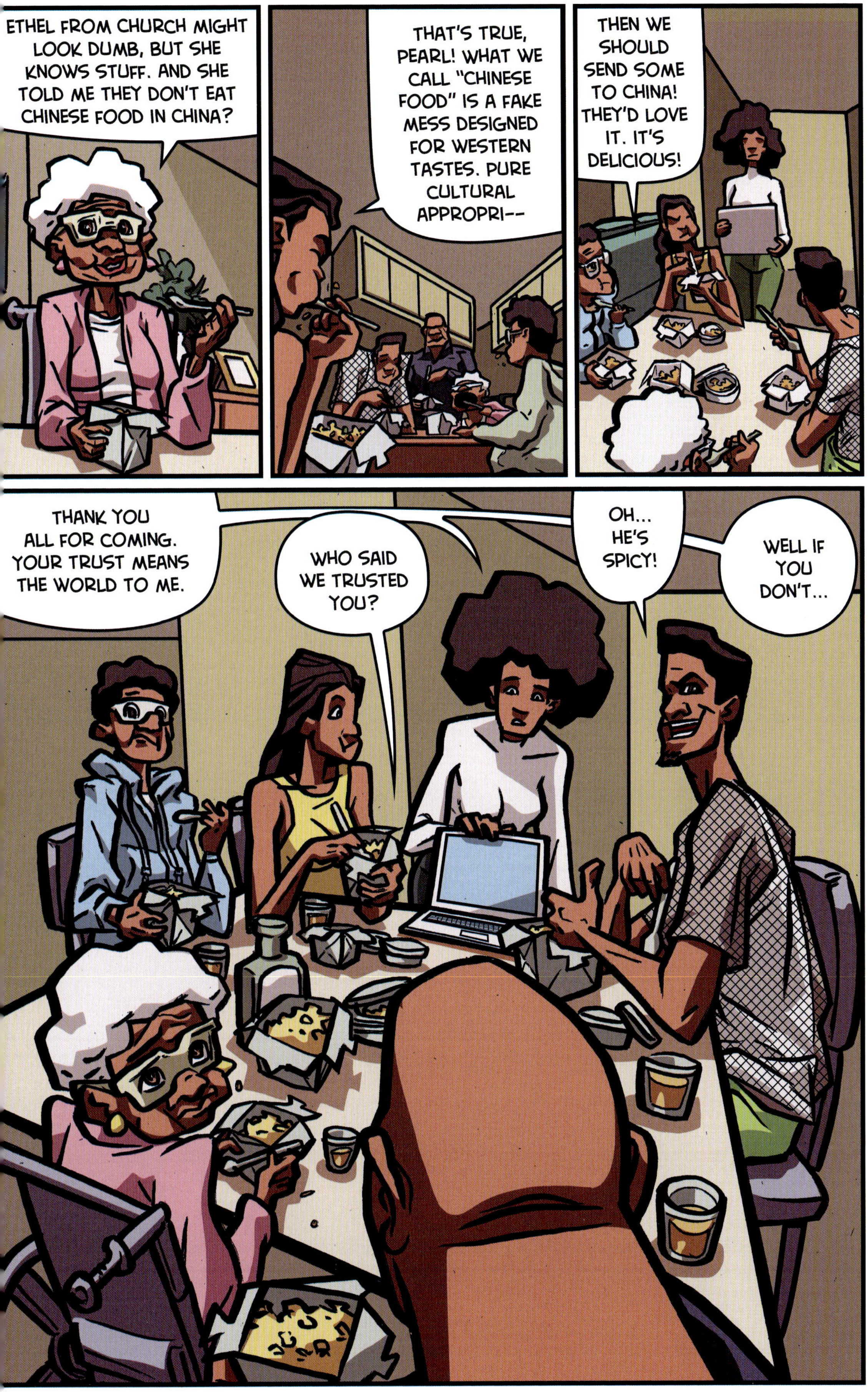
ETHEL FROM CHURCH MIGHT LOOK DUMB, BUT SHE KNOWS STUFF. AND SHE TOLD ME THEY DON'T EAT CHINESE FOOD IN CHINA?
THAT'S TRUE, PEARL! WHAT WE CALL "CHINESE FOOD" IS A FAKE MESS DESIGNED FOR WESTERN TASTES. PURE CULTURAL APPROPRI--
THEN WE SHOULD SEND SOME TO CHINA! THEY'D LOVE IT. IT'S DELICIOUS!
THANK YOU ALL FOR COMING. YOUR TRUST MEANS THE WORLD TO ME.
WHO SAID WE TRUSTED YOU?
OH... HE'S SPICY!
WELL IF YOU DON'T...

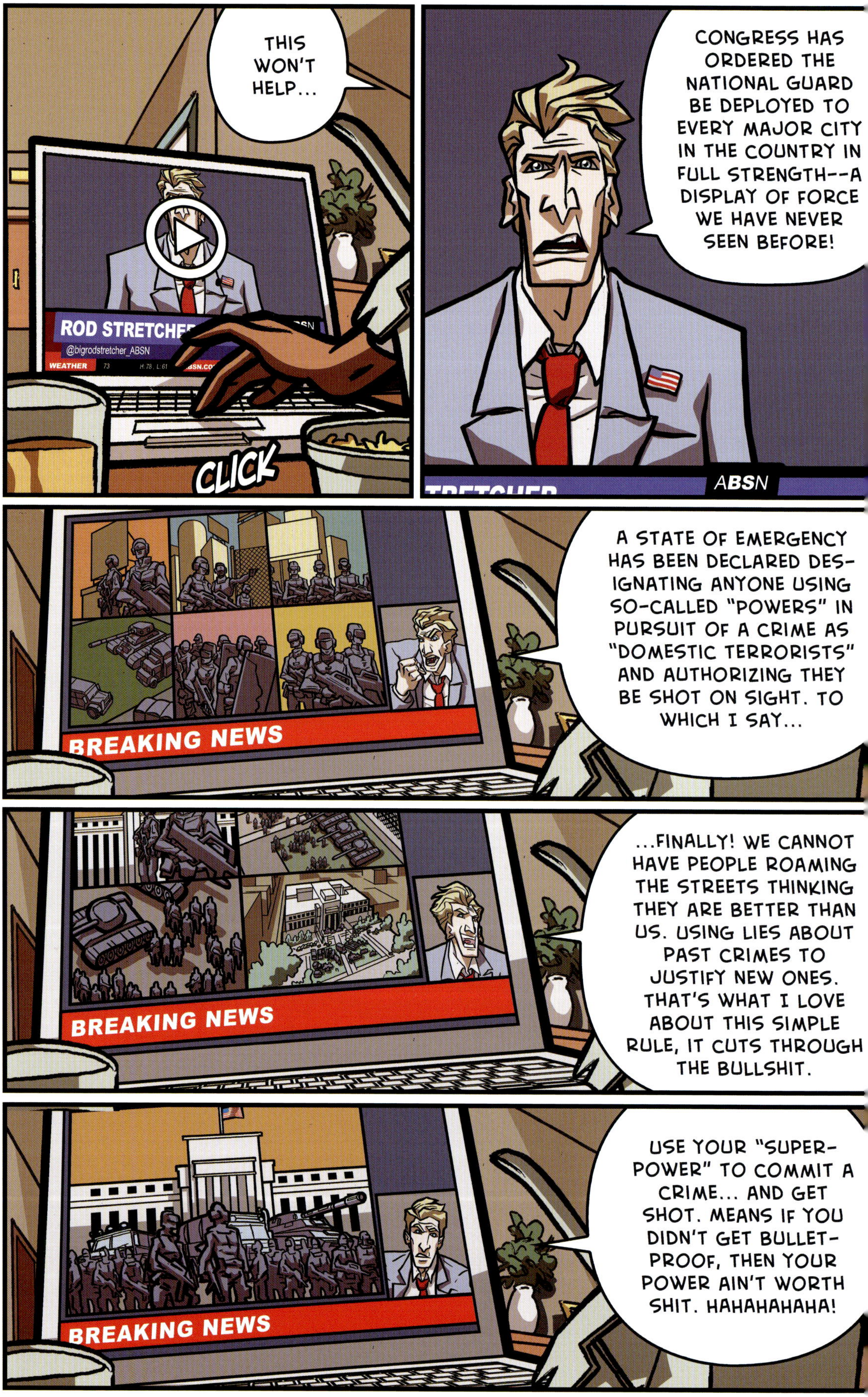
THIS WON'T HELP...
ROD STRETCHER
@bigrodstretcher_ABSN
WEATHER
CLICK
CONGRESS HAS ORDERED THE NATIONAL GUARD BE DEPLOYED TO EVERY MAJOR CITY IN THE COUNTRY IN FULL STRENGTH--A DISPLAY OF FORCE WE HAVE NEVER SEEN BEFORE!
ABSN
BREAKING NEWS
A STATE OF EMERGENCY HAS BEEN DECLARED DESIGNATING ANYONE USING SO-CALLED "POWERS" IN PURSUIT OF A CRIME AS "DOMESTIC TERRORISTS" AND AUTHORIZING THEY BE SHOT ON SIGHT. TO WHICH I SAY...
BREAKING NEWS
...FINALLY! WE CANNOT HAVE PEOPLE ROAMING THE STREETS THINKING THEY ARE BETTER THAN US. USING LIES ABOUT PAST CRIMES TO JUSTIFY NEW ONES. THAT'S WHAT I LOVE ABOUT THIS SIMPLE RULE, IT CUTS THROUGH THE BULLSHIT.
BREAKING NEWS
USE YOUR "SUPER-POWER" TO COMMIT A CRIME... AND GET SHOT. MEANS IF YOU DIDN'T GET BULLET-PROOF, THEN YOUR POWER AIN'T WORTH SHIT. HAHAHAHAHA!

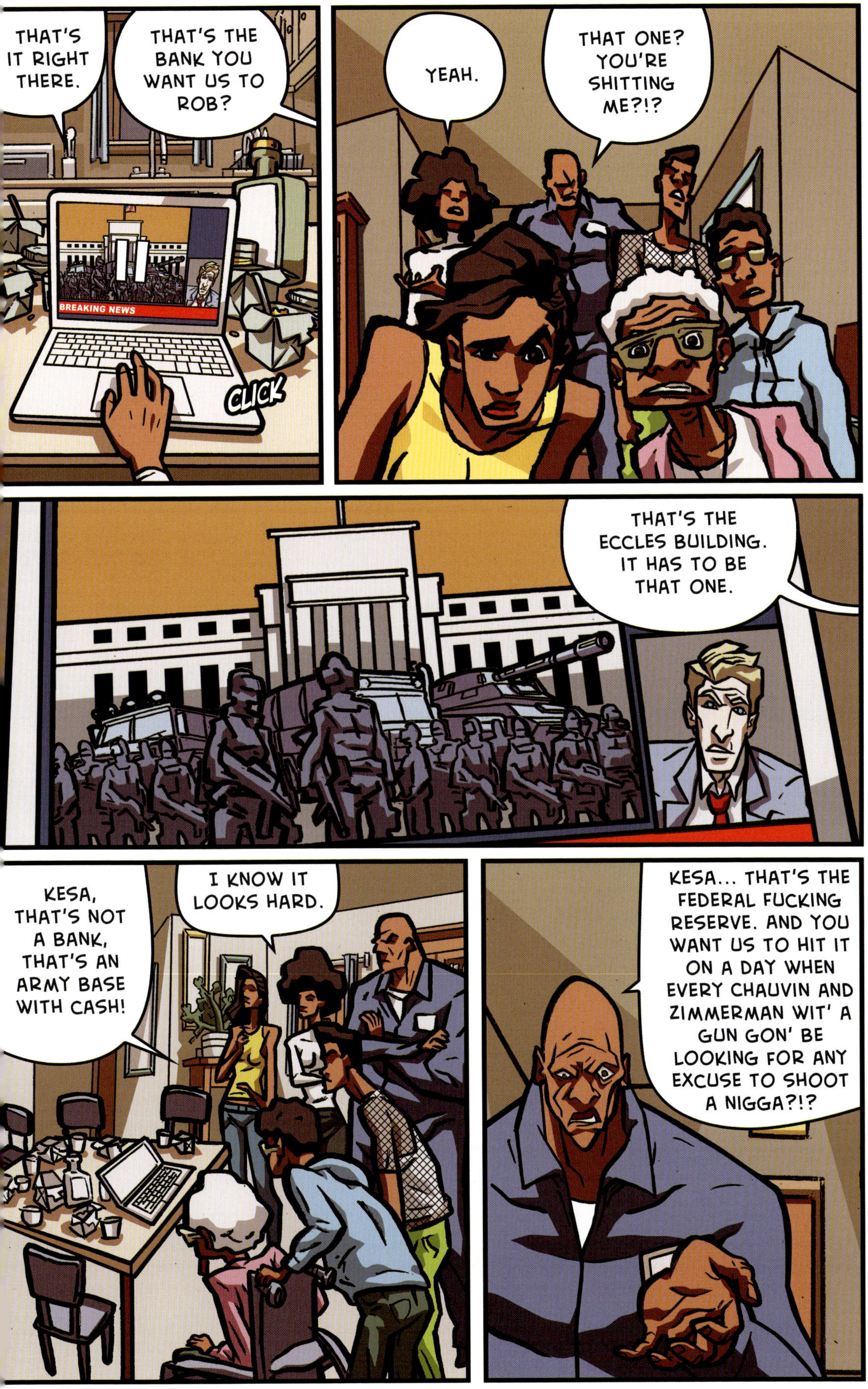
THAT'S IT RIGHT THERE.
THAT'S THE BANK YOU WANT US TO ROB?
BREAKING NEWS
CLICK
YEAH.
THAT ONE? YOU'RE SHITTING ME?!?
THAT'S THE ECCLES BUILDING. IT HAS TO BE THAT ONE.
KESA, THAT'S NOT A BANK, THAT'S AN ARMY BASE WITH CASH!
I KNOW IT LOOKS HARD.
KESA... THAT'S THE FEDERAL FUCKING RESERVE. AND YOU WANT US TO HIT IT ON A DAY WHEN EVERY CHAUVIN AND ZIMMERMAN WIT' A GUN GON' BE LOOKING FOR ANY EXCUSE TO SHOOT A NIGGA?!?

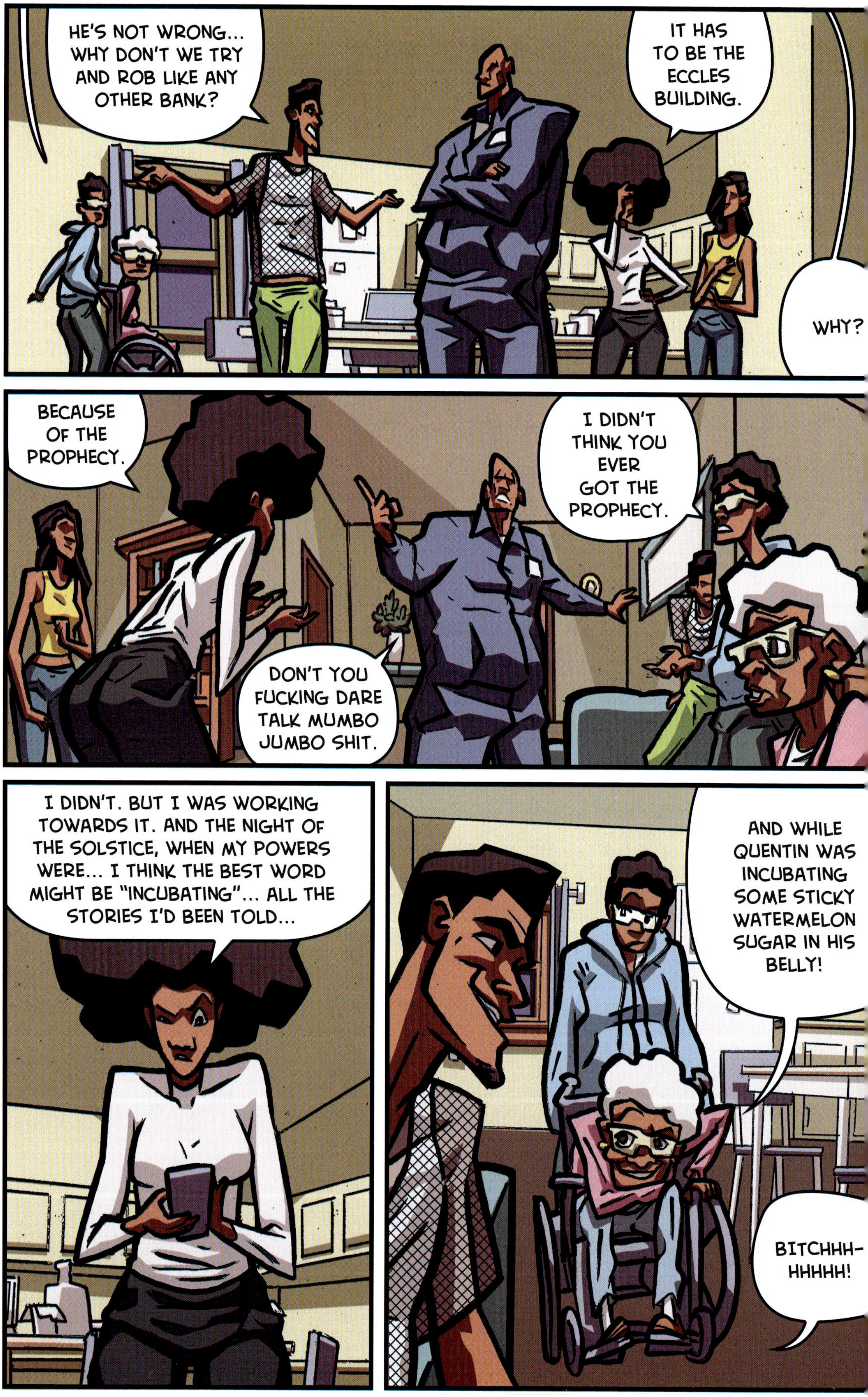
HE'S NOT WRONG... WHY DON'T WE TRY AND ROB LIKE ANY OTHER BANK?
IT HAS TO BE THE ECCLES BUILDING.
WHY?
BECAUSE OF THE PROPHECY.
I DIDN'T THINK YOU EVER GOT THE PROPHECY.
DON'T YOU FUCKING DARE TALK MUMBO JUMBO SHIT.
I DIDN'T. BUT I WAS WORKING TOWARDS IT. AND THE NIGHT OF THE SOLSTICE, WHEN MY POWERS WERE... I THINK THE BEST WORD MIGHT BE "INCUBATING"... ALL THE STORIES I'D BEEN TOLD...
AND WHILE QUENTIN WAS INCUBATING SOME STICKY WATERMELON SUGAR IN HIS BELLY!
BITCHHH-HHHHH!

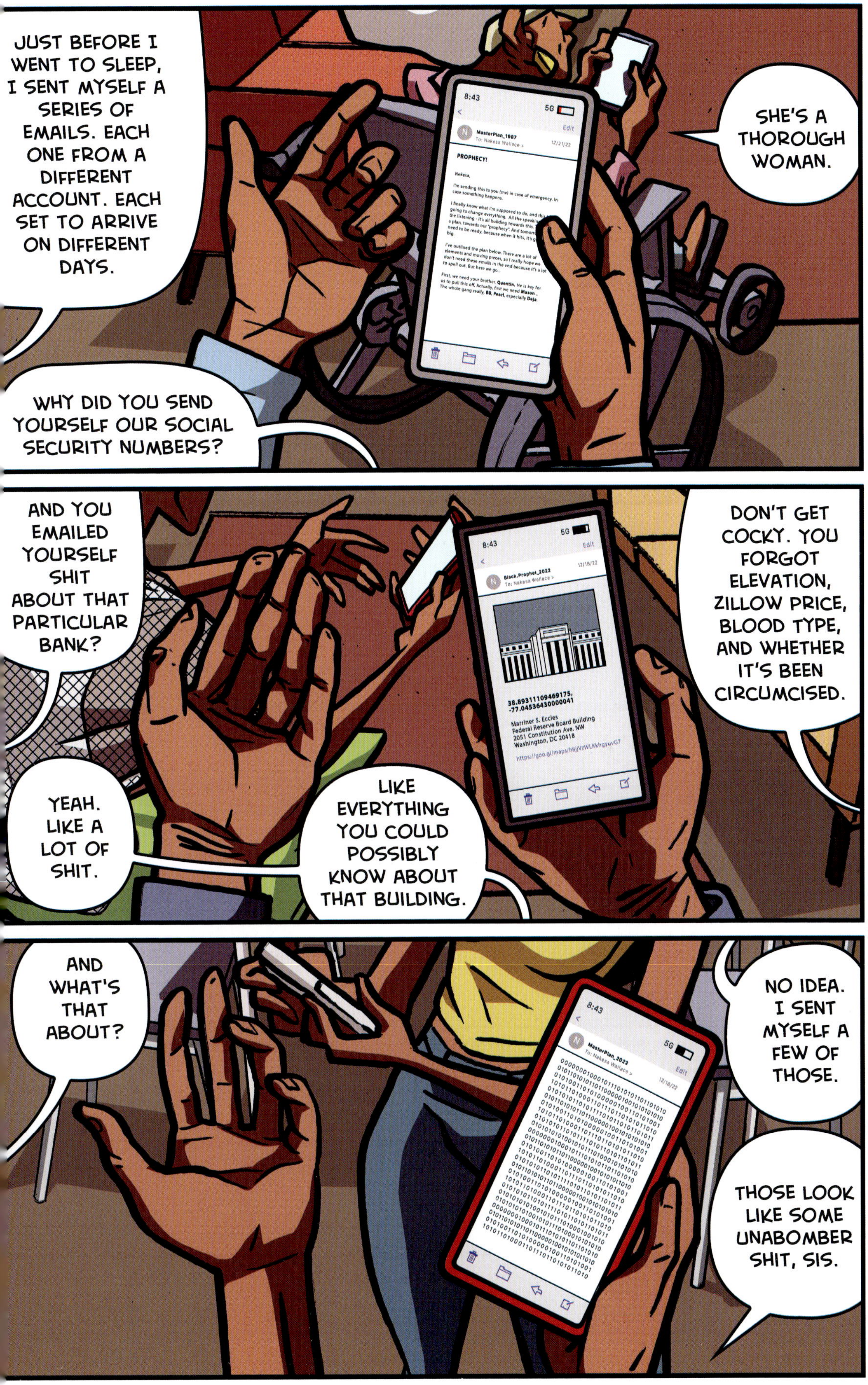
JUST BEFORE I WENT TO SLEEP, I SENT MYSELF A SERIES OF EMAILS. EACH ONE FROM A DIFFERENT ACCOUNT. EACH SET TO ARRIVE ON DIFFERENT DAYS.
SHE'S A THOROUGH WOMAN.
WHY DID YOU SEND YOURSELF OUR SOCIAL SECURITY NUMBERS?
AND YOU EMAILED YOURSELF SHIT ABOUT THAT PARTICULAR BANK?
DON'T GET COCKY. YOU FORGOT ELEVATION, ZILLOW PRICE, BLOOD TYPE, AND WHETHER IT'S BEEN CIRCUMCISED.
YEAH. LIKE A LOT OF SHIT.
LIKE EVERYTHING YOU COULD POSSIBLY KNOW ABOUT THAT BUILDING.
AND WHAT'S THAT ABOUT?
NO IDEA. I SENT MYSELF A FEW OF THOSE.
THOSE LOOK LIKE SOME UNABOMBER SHIT, SIS.

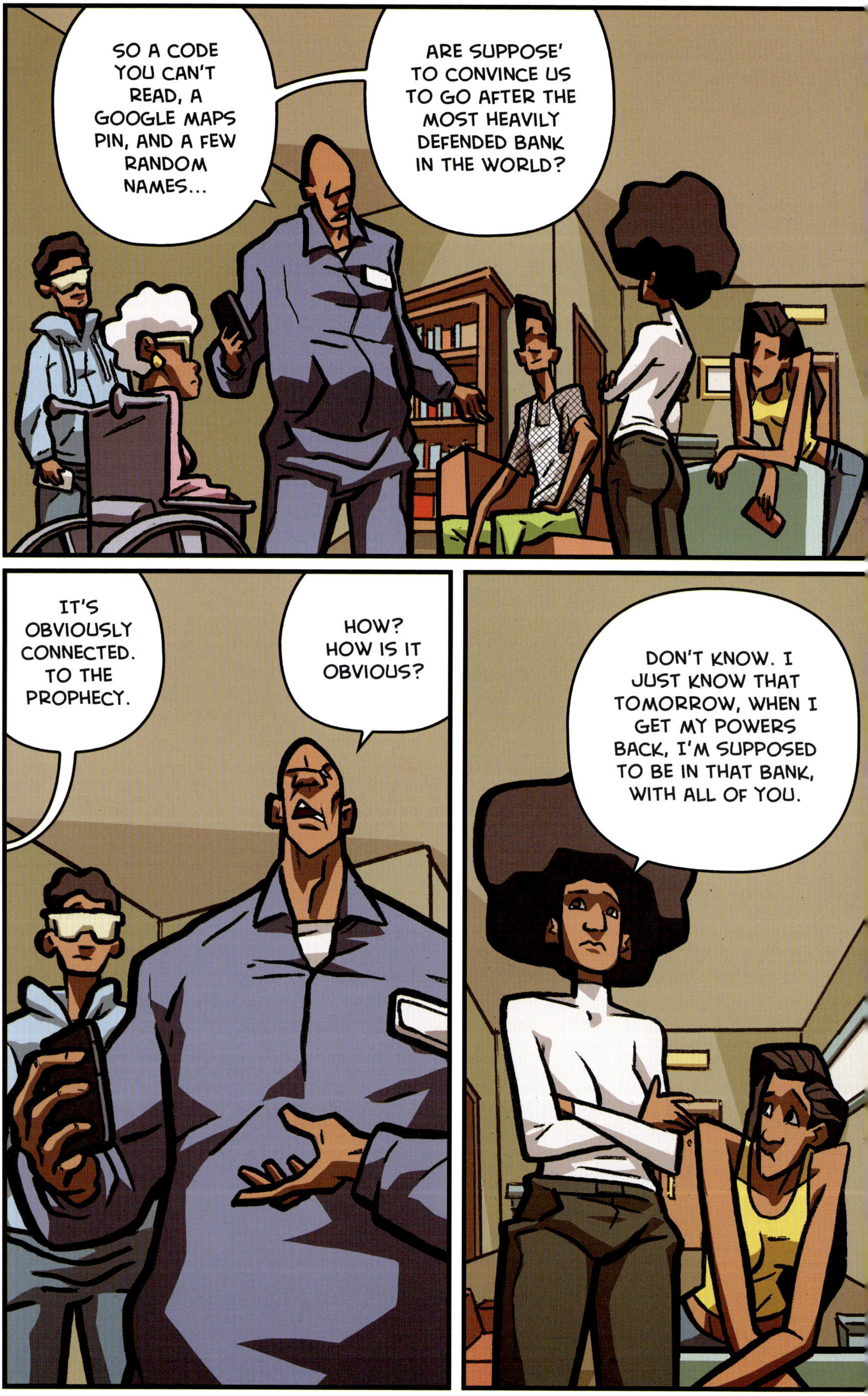
SO A CODE YOU CAN'T READ, A GOOGLE MAPS PIN, AND A FEW RANDOM NAMES...
ARE SUPPOSE' TO CONVINCE US TO GO AFTER THE MOST HEAVILY DEFENDED BANK IN THE WORLD?
IT'S OBVIOUSLY CONNECTED. TO THE PROPHECY.
HOW? HOW IS IT OBVIOUS?
DON'T KNOW. I JUST KNOW THAT TOMORROW, WHEN I GET MY POWERS BACK, I'M SUPPOSED TO BE IN THAT BANK, WITH ALL OF YOU.

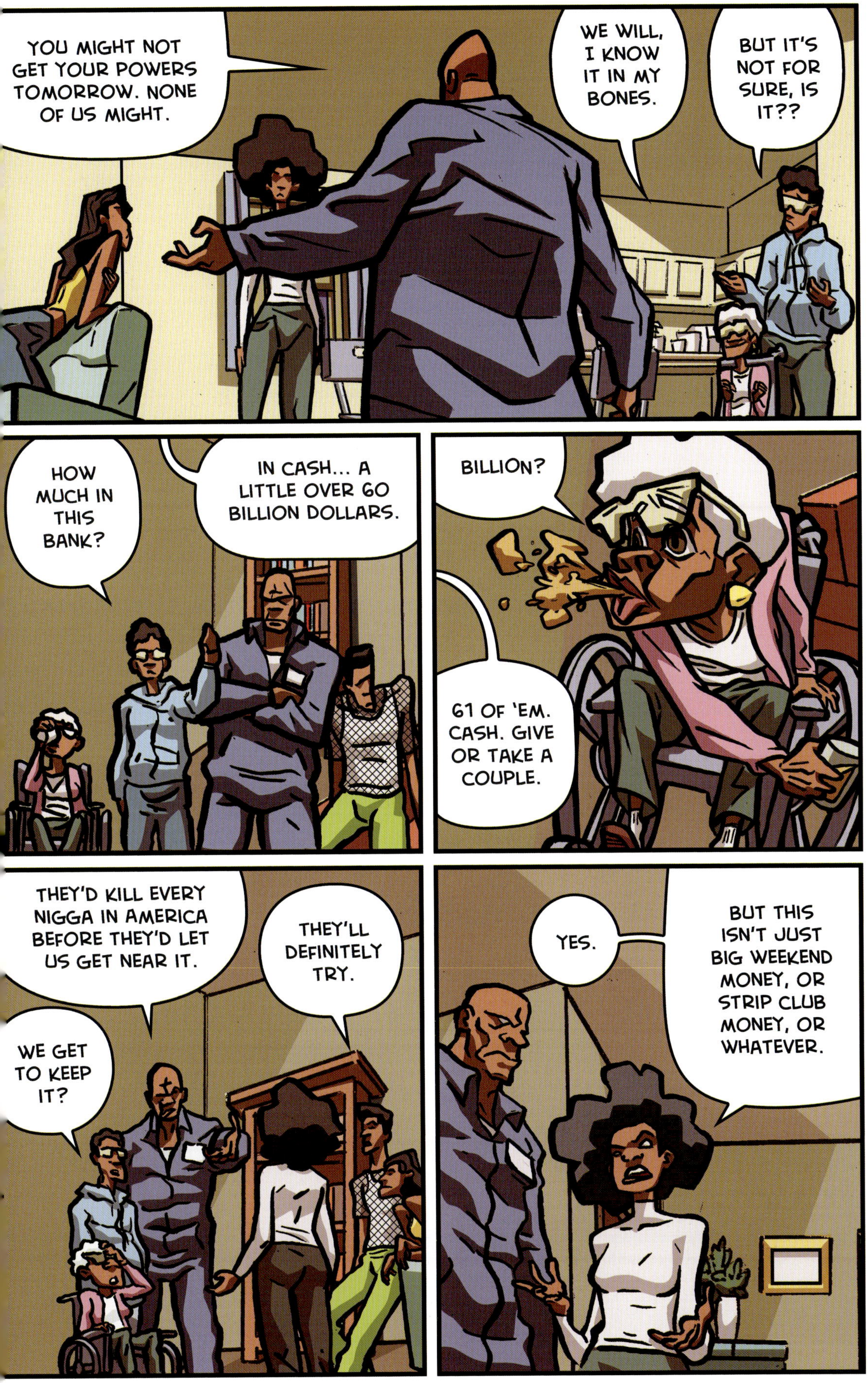
YOU MIGHT NOT GET YOUR POWERS TOMORROW. NONE OF US MIGHT.
WE WILL, I KNOW IT IN MY BONES.
BUT IT'S NOT FOR SURE, IS IT??
HOW MUCH IN THIS BANK?
IN CASH... A LITTLE OVER 60 BILLION DOLLARS.
BILLION?
61 OF 'EM. CASH. GIVE OR TAKE A COUPLE.
THEY'D KILL EVERY NIGGA IN AMERICA BEFORE THEY'D LET US GET NEAR IT.
THEY'LL DEFINITELY TRY.
WE GET TO KEEP IT?
YES.
BUT THIS ISN'T JUST BIG WEEKEND MONEY, OR STRIP CLUB MONEY, OR WHATEVER.

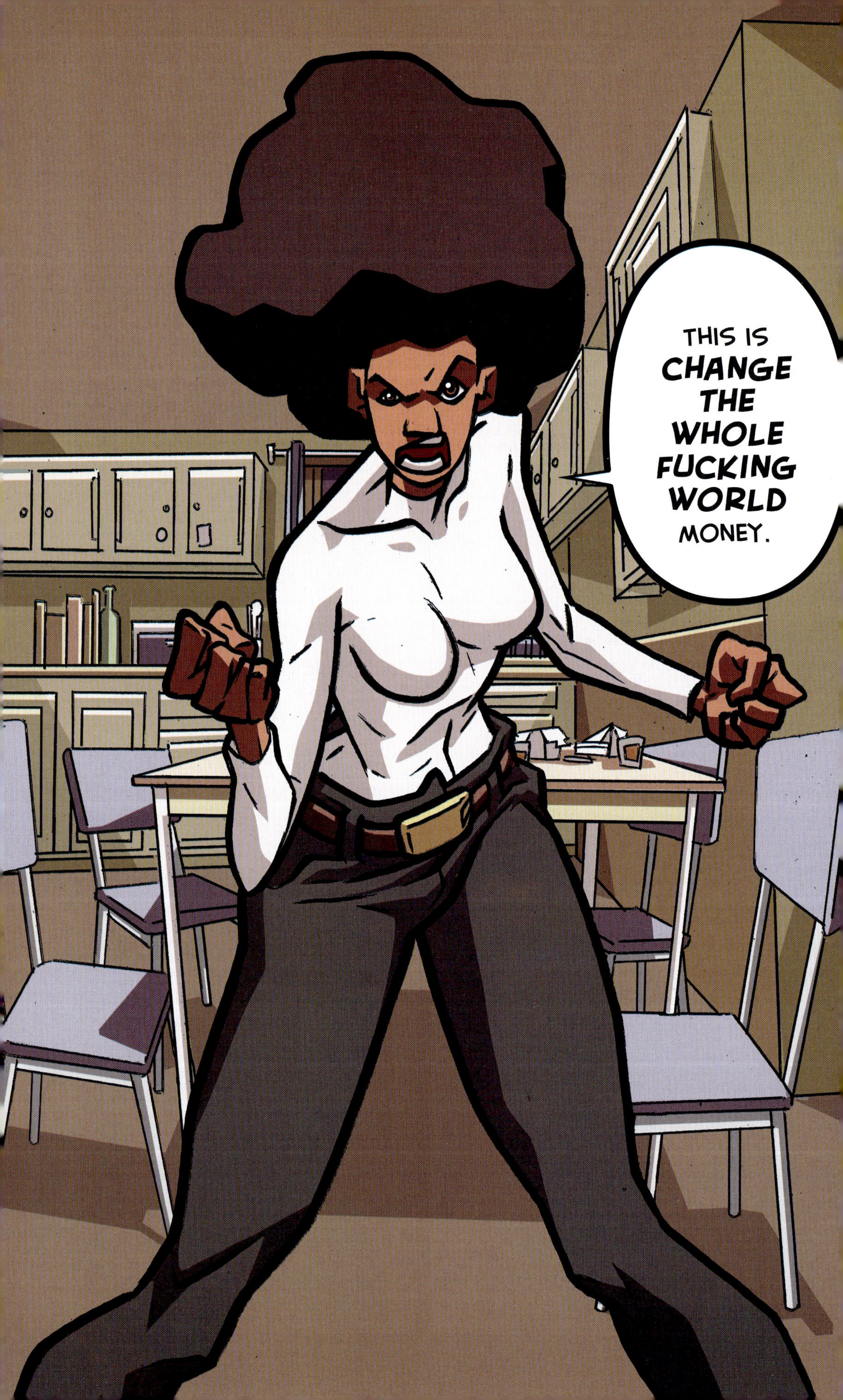
THIS IS CHANGE THE WHOLE FUCKING WORLD MONEY.

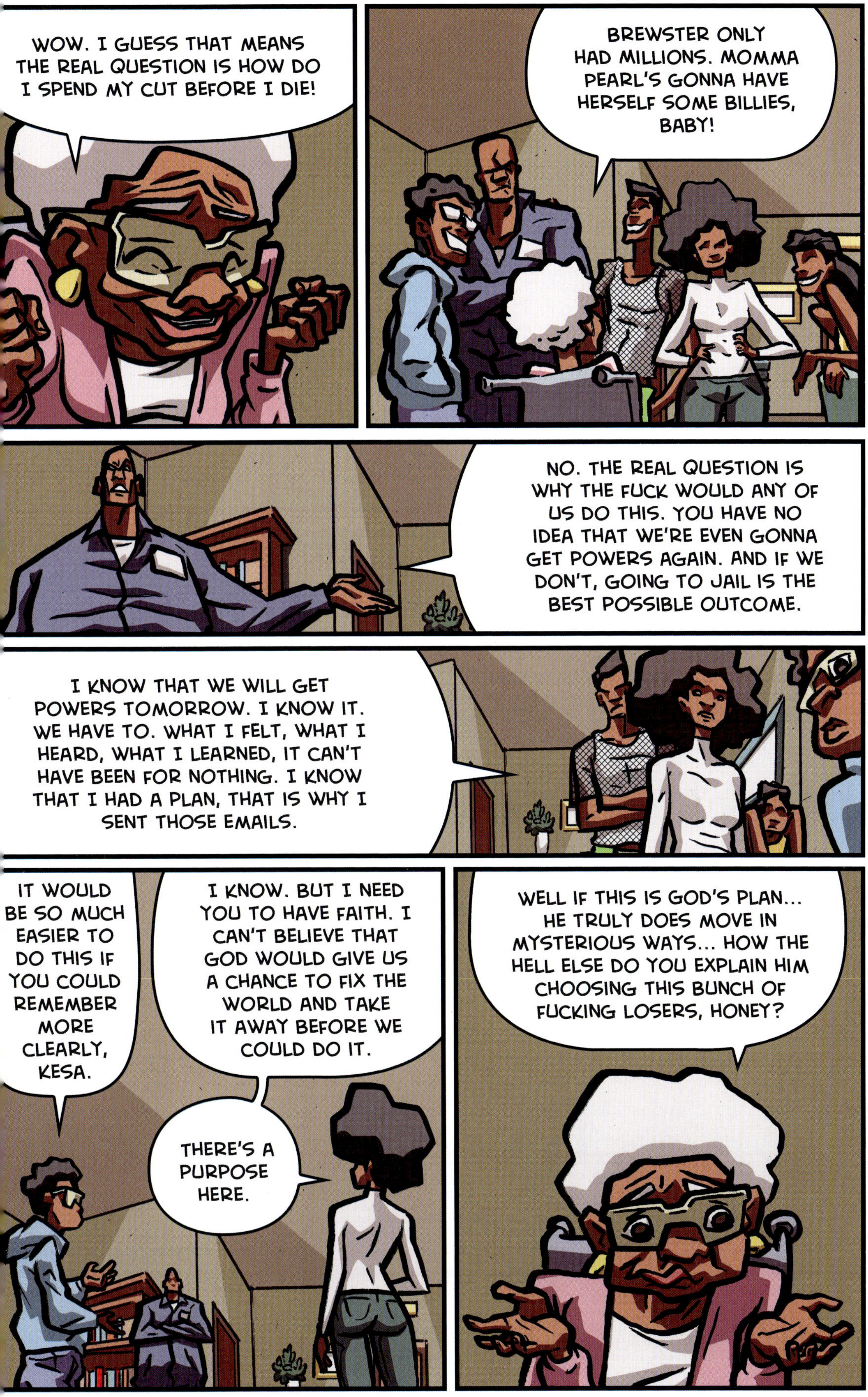
WOW. I GUESS THAT MEANS THE REAL QUESTION IS HOW DO I SPEND MY CUT BEFORE I DIE!
BREWSTER ONLY HAD MILLIONS. MOMMA PEARL'S GONNA HAVE HERSELF SOME BILLIES, BABY!
NO. THE REAL QUESTION IS WHY THE FUCK WOULD ANY OF US DO THIS. YOU HAVE NO IDEA THAT WE'RE EVEN GONNA GET POWERS AGAIN. AND IF WE DON'T, GOING TO JAIL IS THE BEST POSSIBLE OUTCOME.
I KNOW THAT WE WILL GET POWERS TOMORROW. I KNOW IT. WE HAVE TO. WHAT I FELT, WHAT I HEARD, WHAT I LEARNED, IT CAN'T HAVE BEEN FOR NOTHING. I KNOW THAT I HAD A PLAN, THAT IS WHY I SENT THOSE EMAILS.
IT WOULD BE SO MUCH EASIER TO DO THIS IF YOU COULD REMEMBER MORE CLEARLY, KESA.
I KNOW. BUT I NEED YOU TO HAVE FAITH. I CAN'T BELIEVE THAT GOD WOULD GIVE US A CHANCE TO FIX THE WORLD AND TAKE IT AWAY BEFORE WE COULD DO IT.
THERE'S A PURPOSE HERE.
WELL IF THIS IS GOD'S PLAN... HE TRULY DOES MOVE IN MYSTERIOUS WAYS... HOW THE HELL ELSE DO YOU EXPLAIN HIM CHOOSING THIS BUNCH OF FUCKING LOSERS, HONEY?

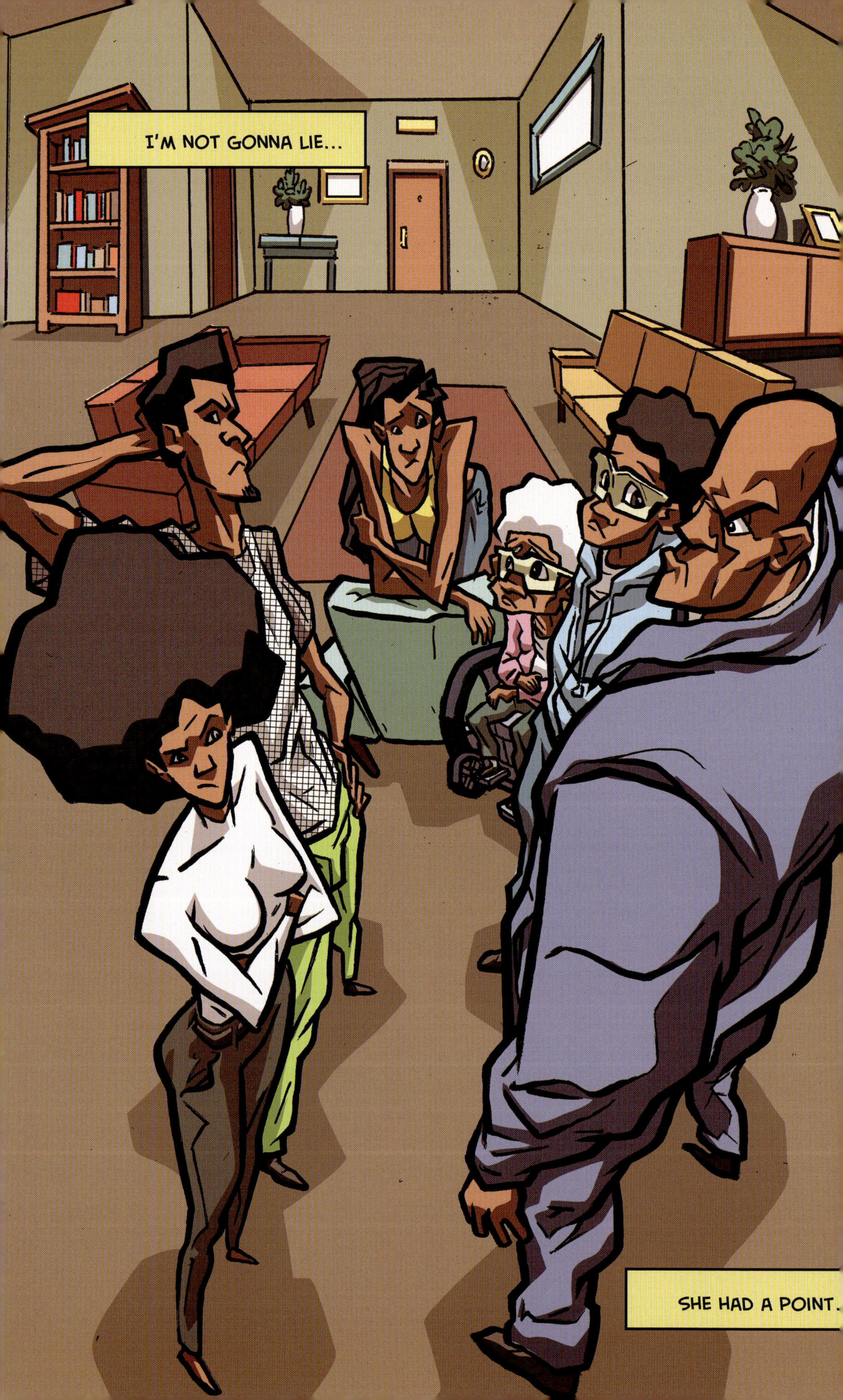
I'M NOT GONNA LIE...
SHE HAD A POINT.

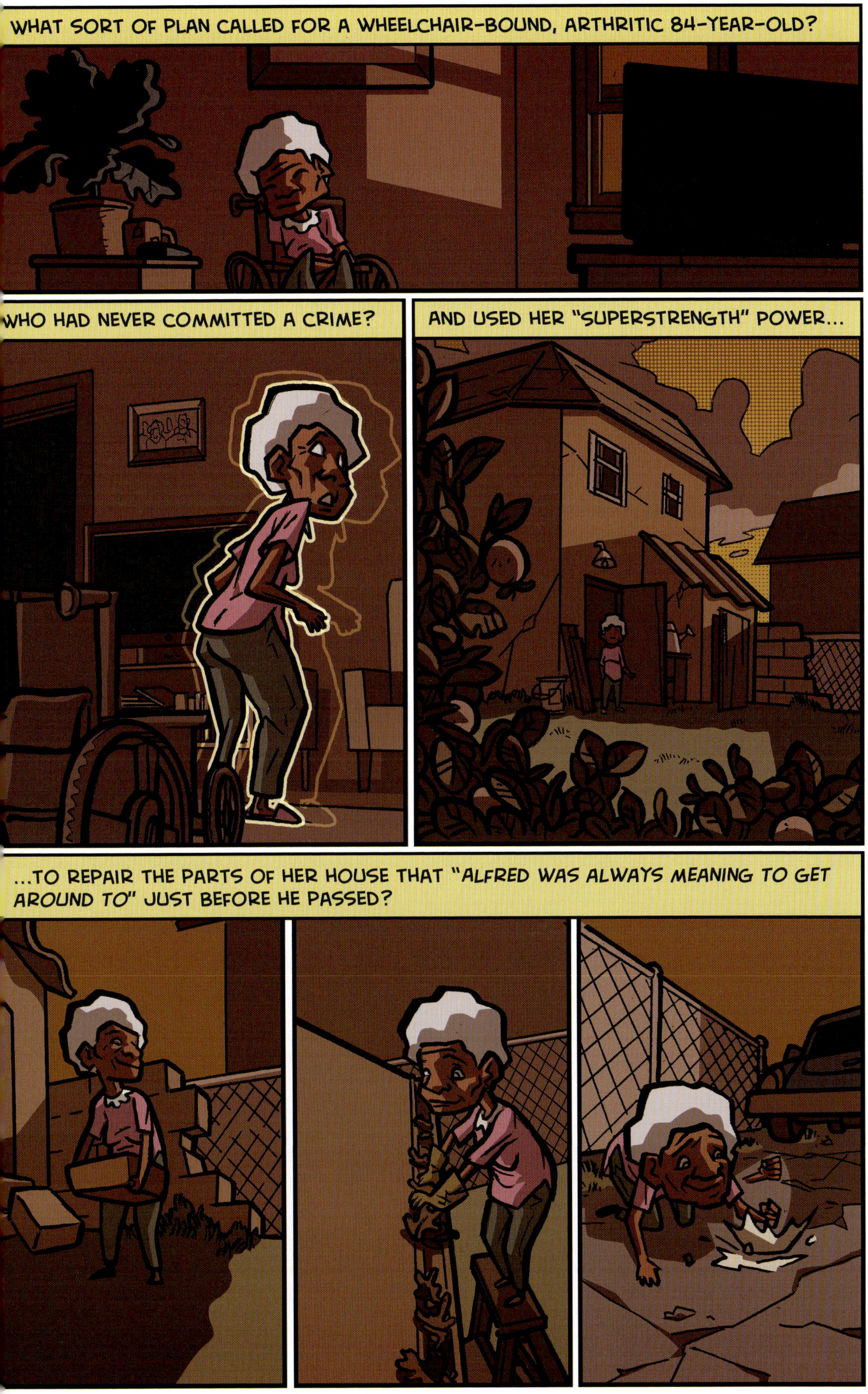
WHAT SORT OF PLAN CALLED FOR A WHEELCHAIR-BOUND, ARTHRITIC 84-YEAR-OLD?
WHO HAD NEVER COMMITTED A CRIME?
AND USED HER "SUPERSTRENGTH" POWER...
...TO REPAIR THE PARTS OF HER HOUSE THAT "ALFRED WAS ALWAYS MEANING TO GET AROUND TO" JUST BEFORE HE PASSED?

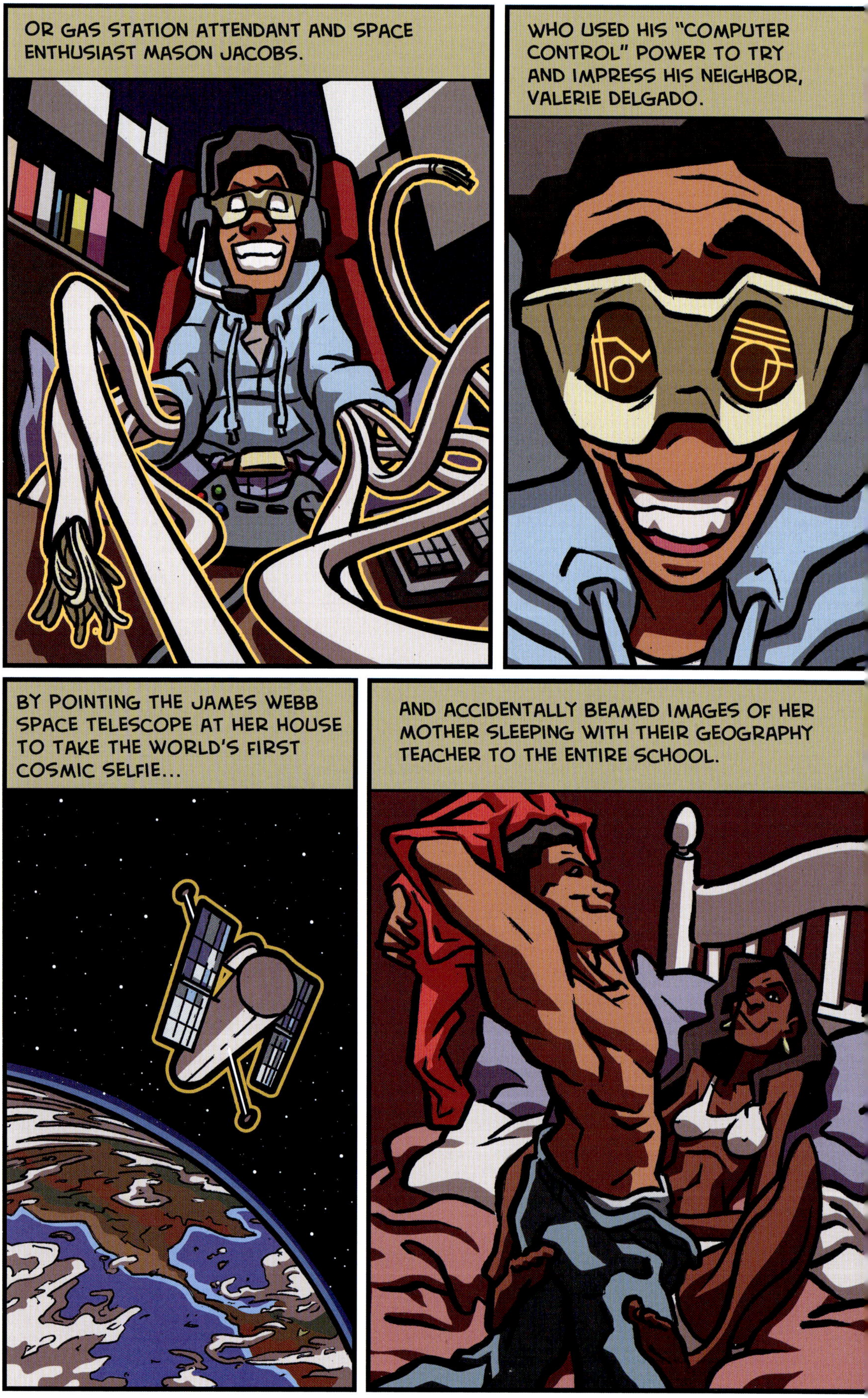
OR GAS STATION ATTENDANT AND SPACE ENTHUSIAST MASON JACOBS.
WHO USED HIS "COMPUTER CONTROL" POWER TO TRY AND IMPRESS HIS NEIGHBOR, VALERIE DELGADO.
BY POINTING THE JAMES WEBB SPACE TELESCOPE AT HER HOUSE TO TAKE THE WORLD'S FIRST COSMIC SELFIE...
AND ACCIDENTALLY BEAMED IMAGES OF HER MOTHER SLEEPING WITH THEIR GEOGRAPHY TEACHER TO THE ENTIRE SCHOOL.

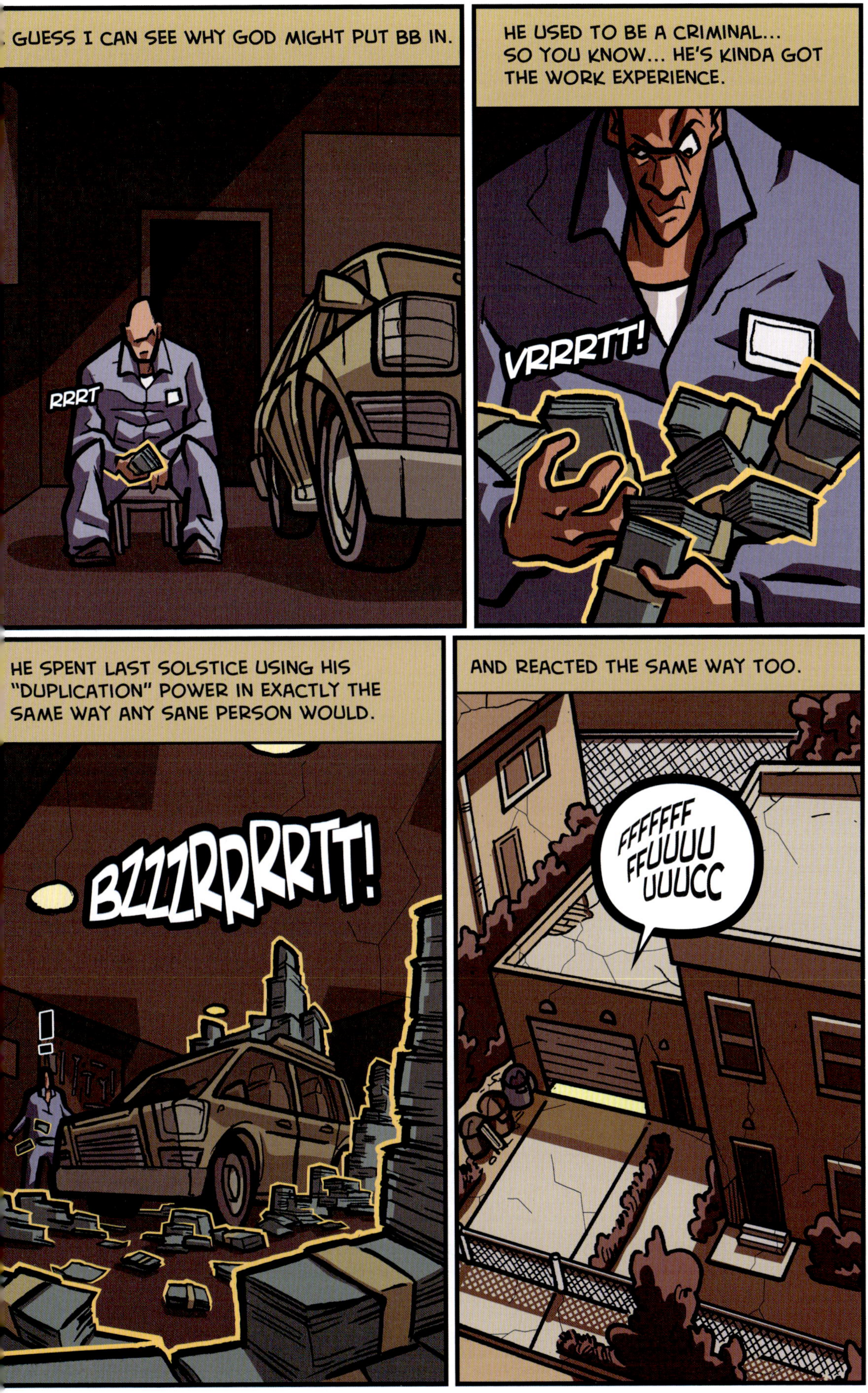
GUESS I CAN SEE WHY GOD MIGHT PUT BB IN.
RRRT
HE USED TO BE A CRIMINAL... SO YOU KNOW... HE'S KINDA GOT THE WORK EXPERIENCE.
VRRRTT!
HE SPENT LAST SOLSTICE USING HIS "DUPLICATION" POWER IN EXACTLY THE SAME WAY ANY SANE PERSON WOULD.
BZZZRRRRTT!
!
AND REACTED THE SAME WAY TOO.
FFFFFFF FFUUUU UUUCC

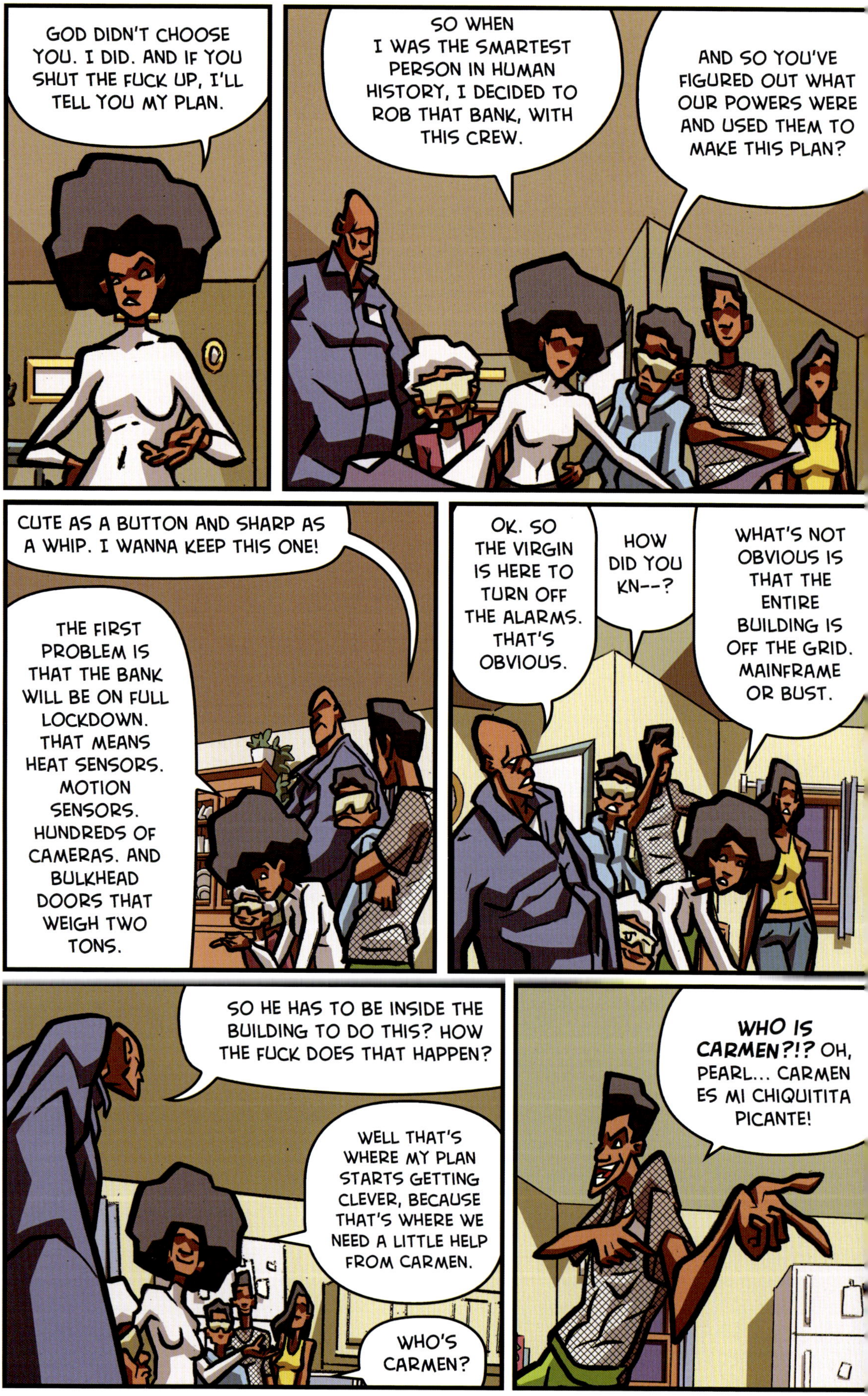
GOD DIDN'T CHOOSE YOU. I DID. AND IF YOU SHUT THE FUCK UP, I'LL TELL YOU MY PLAN.
SO WHEN I WAS THE SMARTEST PERSON IN HUMAN HISTORY, I DECIDED TO ROB THAT BANK, WITH THIS CREW.
AND SO YOU'VE FIGURED OUT WHAT OUR POWERS WERE AND USED THEM TO MAKE THIS PLAN?
CUTE AS A BUTTON AND SHARP AS A WHIP. I WANNA KEEP THIS ONE!
THE FIRST PROBLEM IS THAT THE BANK WILL BE ON FULL LOCKDOWN. THAT MEANS HEAT SENSORS. MOTION SENSORS. HUNDREDS OF CAMERAS. AND BULKHEAD DOORS THAT WEIGH TWO TONS.
OK. SO THE VIRGIN IS HERE TO TURN OFF THE ALARMS. THAT'S OBVIOUS.
HOW DID YOU KN--?
WHAT'S NOT OBVIOUS IS THAT THE ENTIRE BUILDING IS OFF THE GRID. MAINFRAME OR BUST.
SO HE HAS TO BE INSIDE THE BUILDING TO DO THIS? HOW THE FUCK DOES THAT HAPPEN?
WELL THAT'S WHERE MY PLAN STARTS GETTING CLEVER, BECAUSE THAT'S WHERE WE NEED A LITTLE HELP FROM CARMEN.
WHO'S CARMEN?
WHO IS CARMEN?!? OH, PEARL... CARMEN ES MI CHIQUITITA PICANTE!

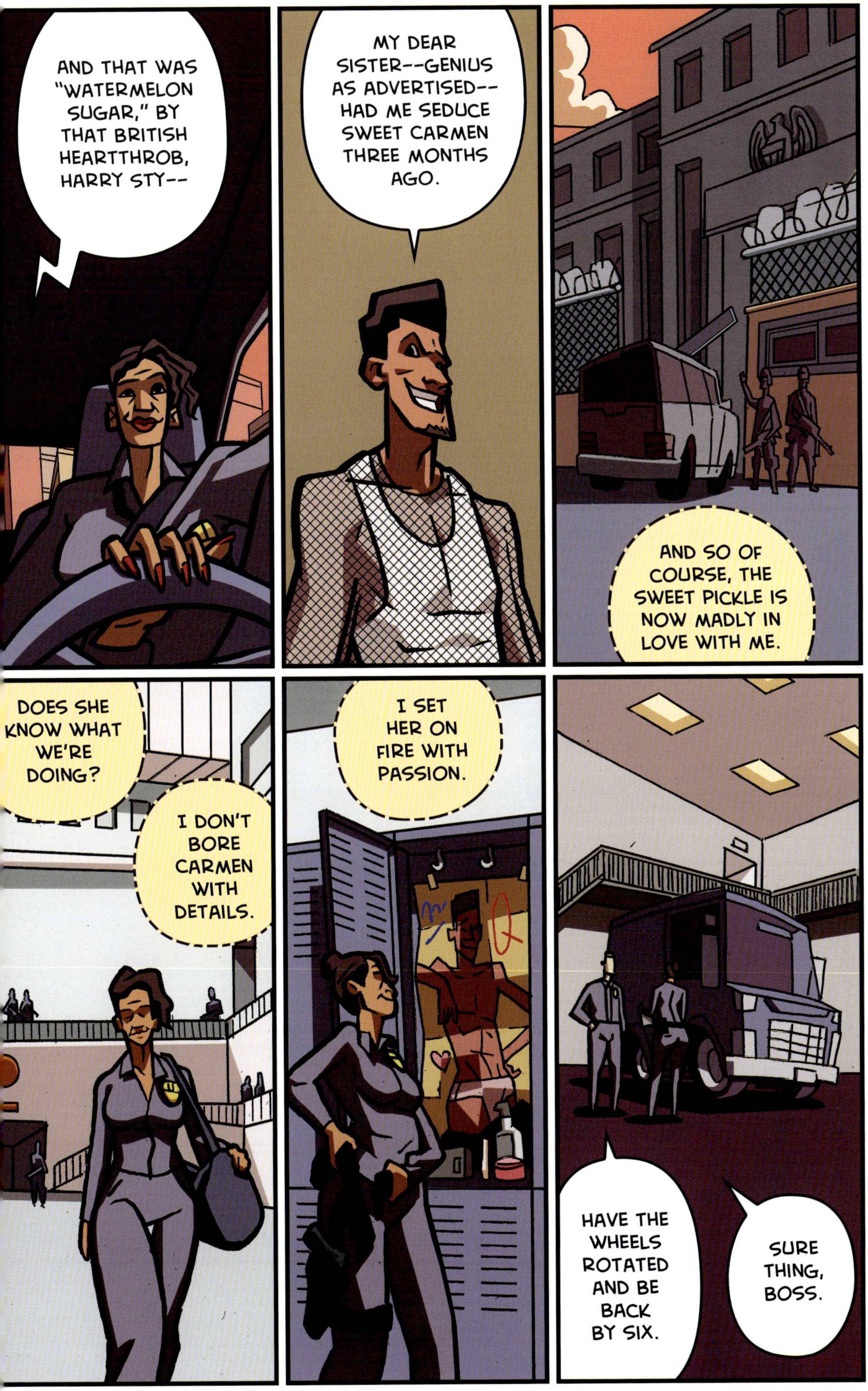
AND THAT WAS "WATERMELON SUGAR," BY THAT BRITISH HEARTTHROB, HARRY STY--
MY DEAR SISTER--GENIUS AS ADVERTISED--HAD ME SEDUCE SWEET CARMEN THREE MONTHS AGO.
AND SO OF COURSE, THE SWEET PICKLE IS NOW MADLY IN LOVE WITH ME.
DOES SHE KNOW WHAT WE'RE DOING?
I DON'T BORE CARMEN WITH DETAILS.
I SET HER ON FIRE WITH PASSION.
HAVE THE WHEELS ROTATED AND BE BACK BY SIX.
SURE THING, BOSS.

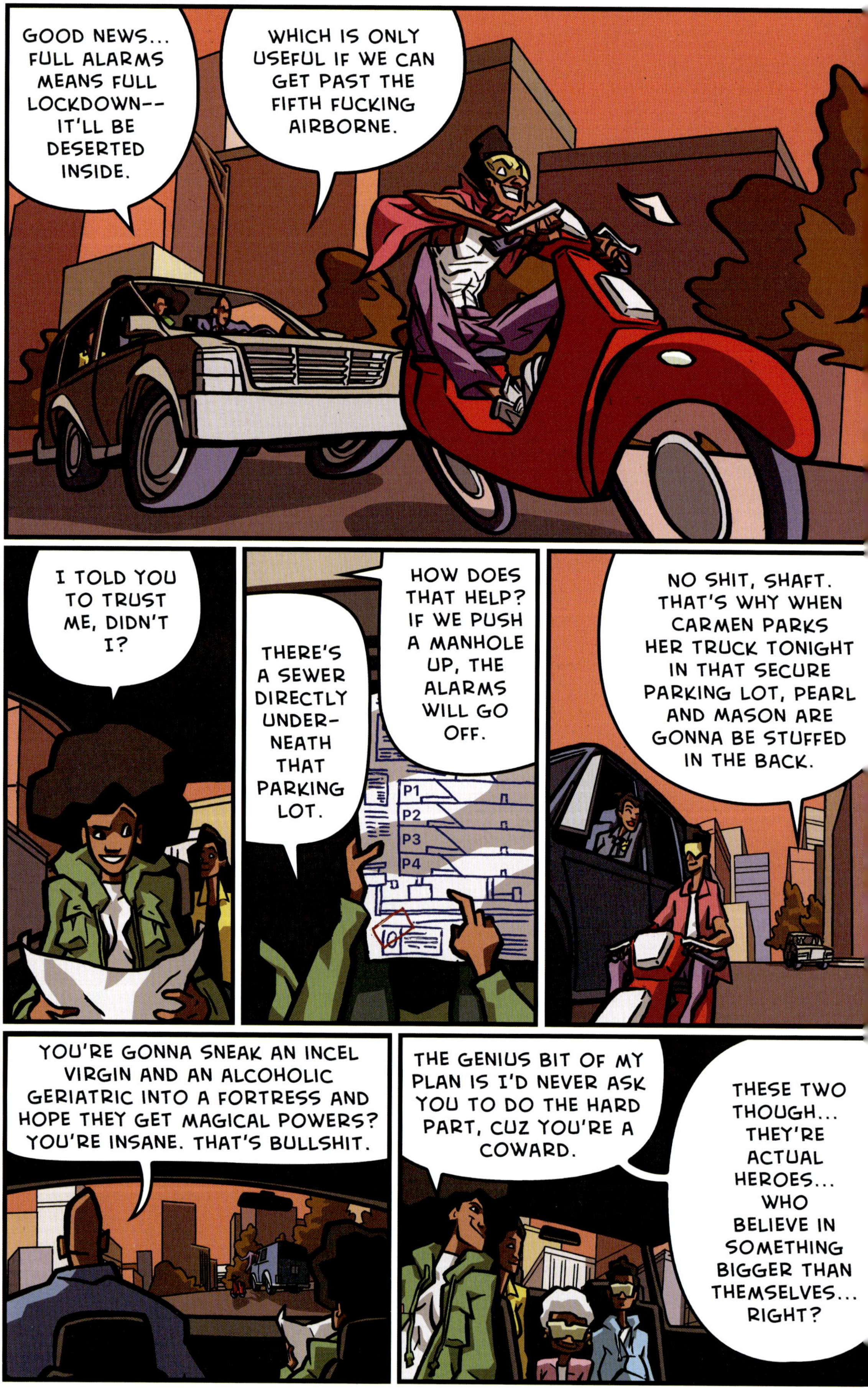
GOOD NEWS... FULL ALARMS MEANS FULL LOCKDOWN-- IT'LL BE DESERTED INSIDE.
WHICH IS ONLY USEFUL IF WE CAN GET PAST THE FIFTH FUCKING AIRBORNE.
I TOLD YOU TO TRUST ME, DIDN'T I?
THERE'S A SEWER DIRECTLY UNDER-NEATH THAT PARKING LOT.
HOW DOES THAT HELP? IF WE PUSH A MANHOLE UP, THE ALARMS WILL GO OFF.
P1
P2
P3
P4
NO SHIT, SHAFT. THAT'S WHY WHEN CARMEN PARKS HER TRUCK TONIGHT IN THAT SECURE PARKING LOT, PEARL AND MASON ARE GONNA BE STUFFED IN THE BACK.
YOU'RE GONNA SNEAK AN INCEL VIRGIN AND AN ALCOHOLIC GERIATRIC INTO A FORTRESS AND HOPE THEY GET MAGICAL POWERS? YOU'RE INSANE. THAT'S BULLSHIT.
THE GENIUS BIT OF MY PLAN IS I'D NEVER ASK YOU TO DO THE HARD PART, CUZ YOU'RE A COWARD.
THESE TWO THOUGH... THEY'RE ACTUAL HEROES... WHO BELIEVE IN SOMETHING BIGGER THAN THEMSELVES... RIGHT?

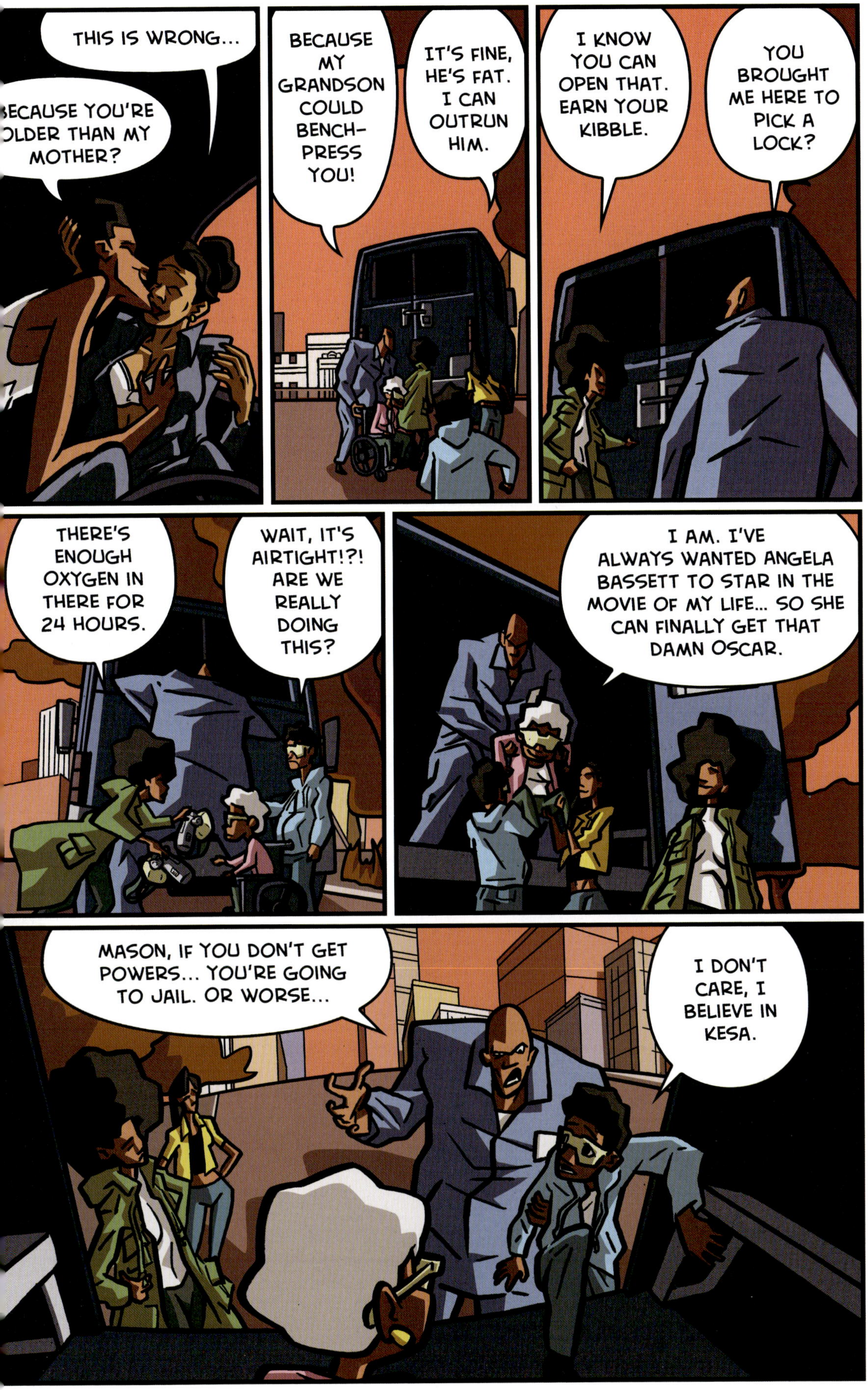
THIS IS WRONG...
BECAUSE YOU'RE OLDER THAN MY MOTHER?
BECAUSE MY GRANDSON COULD BENCH-PRESS YOU!
IT'S FINE, HE'S FAT. I CAN OUTRUN HIM.
I KNOW YOU CAN OPEN THAT. EARN YOUR KIBBLE.
YOU BROUGHT ME HERE TO PICK A LOCK?
THERE'S ENOUGH OXYGEN IN THERE FOR 24 HOURS.
WAIT, IT'S AIRTIGHT!?! ARE WE REALLY DOING THIS?
I AM. I'VE ALWAYS WANTED ANGELA BASSETT TO STAR IN THE MOVIE OF MY LIFE... SO SHE CAN FINALLY GET THAT DAMN OSCAR.
MASON, IF YOU DON'T GET POWERS... YOU'RE GOING TO JAIL. OR WORSE...
I DON'T CARE, I BELIEVE IN KESA.

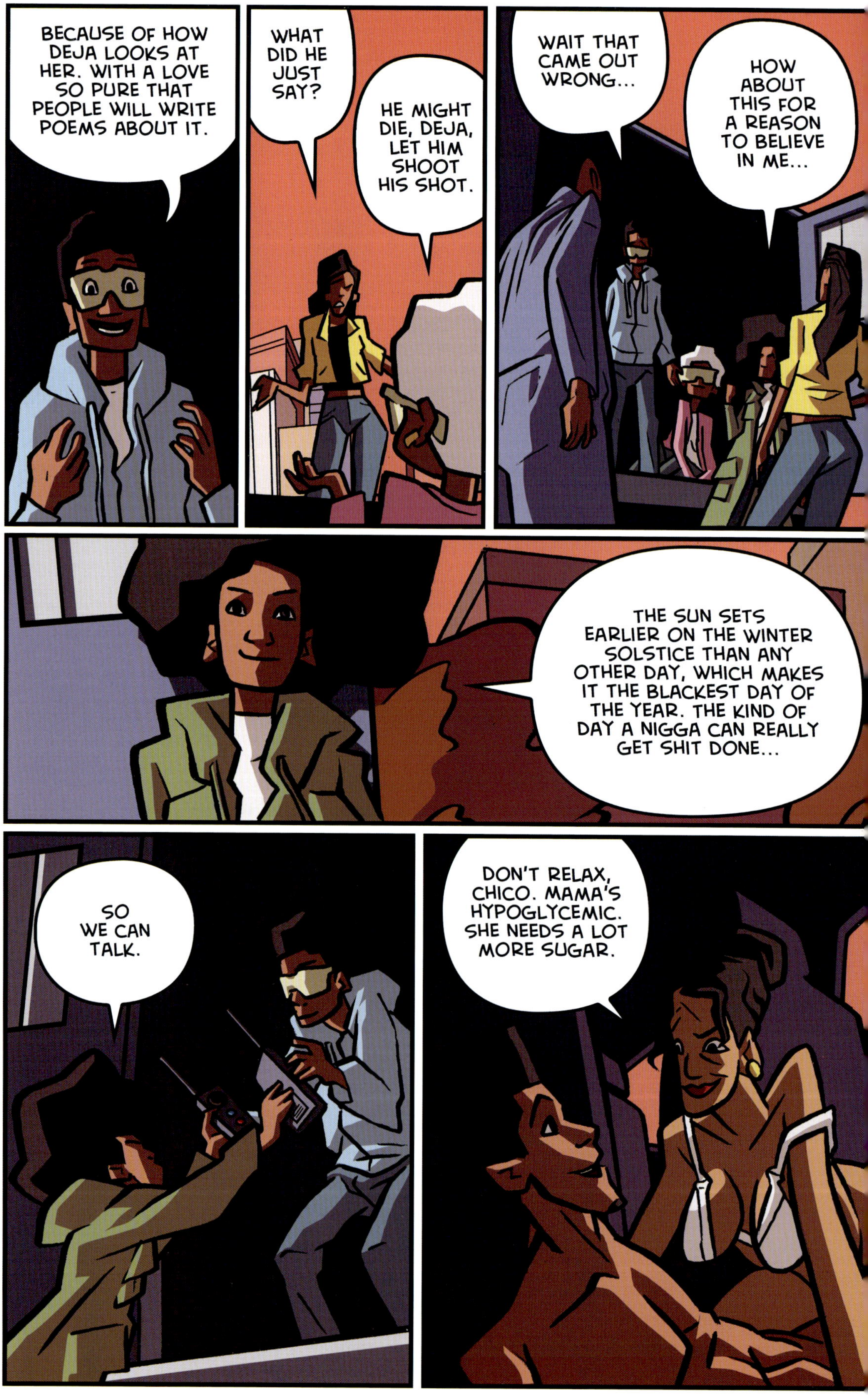
BECAUSE OF HOW DEJA LOOKS AT HER. WITH A LOVE SO PURE THAT PEOPLE WILL WRITE POEMS ABOUT IT.
WHAT DID HE JUST SAY?
HE MIGHT DIE, DEJA, LET HIM SHOOT HIS SHOT.
WAIT THAT CAME OUT WRONG...
HOW ABOUT THIS FOR A REASON TO BELIEVE IN ME...
THE SUN SETS EARLIER ON THE WINTER SOLSTICE THAN ANY OTHER DAY, WHICH MAKES IT THE BLACKEST DAY OF THE YEAR. THE KIND OF DAY A NIGGA CAN REALLY GET SHIT DONE...
SO WE CAN TALK.
DON'T RELAX, CHICO. MAMA'S HYPOGLYCEMIC. SHE NEEDS A LOT MORE SUGAR.

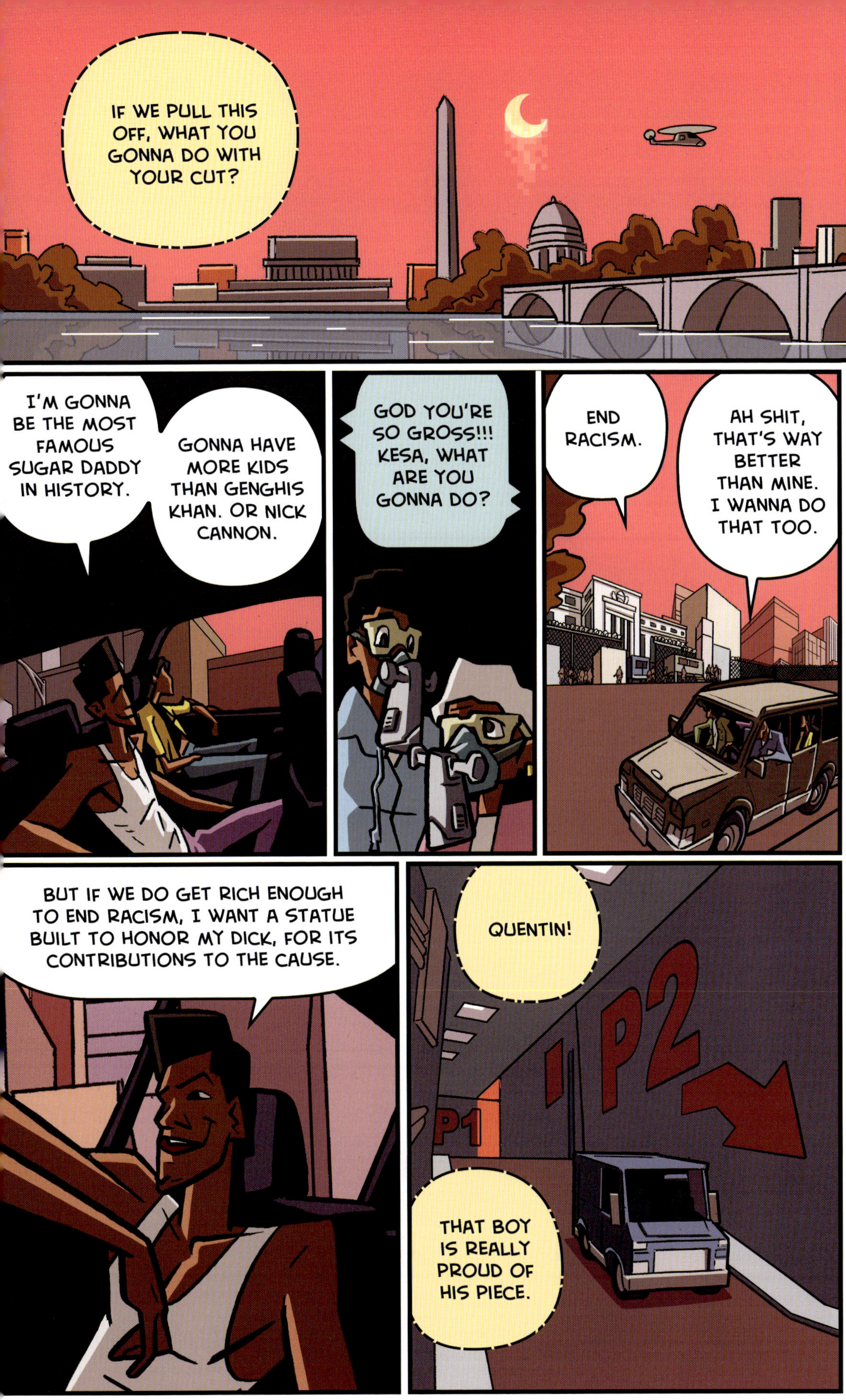
IF WE PULL THIS OFF, WHAT YOU GONNA DO WITH YOUR CUT?
I'M GONNA BE THE MOST FAMOUS SUGAR DADDY IN HISTORY.
GONNA HAVE MORE KIDS THAN GENGHIS KHAN. OR NICK CANNON.
GOD YOU'RE SO GROSS!!! KESA, WHAT ARE YOU GONNA DO?
END RACISM.
AH SHIT, THAT'S WAY BETTER THAN MINE. I WANNA DO THAT TOO.
BUT IF WE DO GET RICH ENOUGH TO END RACISM, I WANT A STATUE BUILT TO HONOR MY DICK, FOR ITS CONTRIBUTIONS TO THE CAUSE.
QUENTIN!
P2
P1
THAT BOY IS REALLY PROUD OF HIS PIECE.

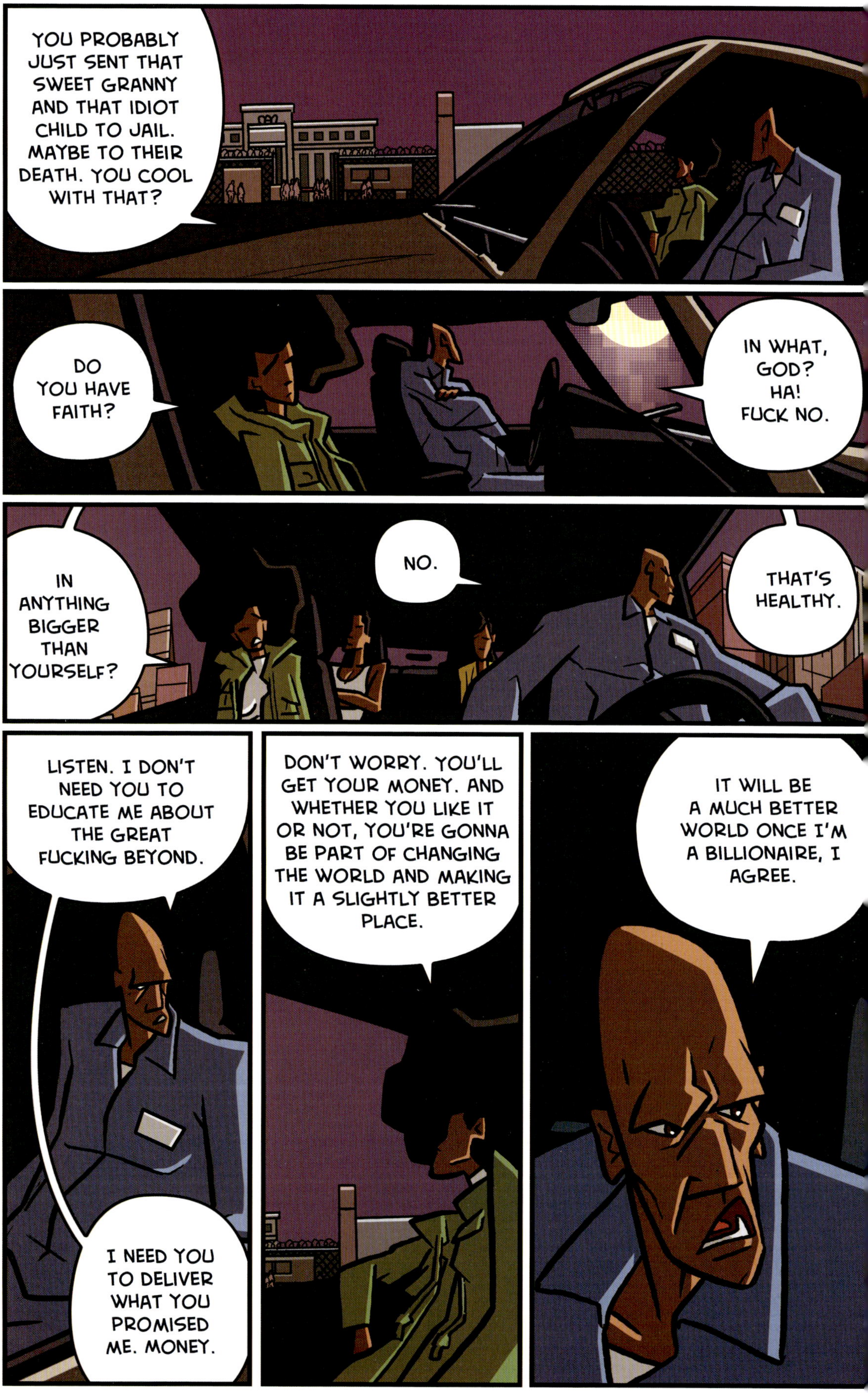
YOU PROBABLY JUST SENT THAT SWEET GRANNY AND THAT IDIOT CHILD TO JAIL. MAYBE TO THEIR DEATH. YOU COOL WITH THAT?
DO YOU HAVE FAITH?
IN WHAT, GOD? HA! FUCK NO.
IN ANYTHING BIGGER THAN YOURSELF?
NO.
THAT'S HEALTHY.
LISTEN. I DON'T NEED YOU TO EDUCATE ME ABOUT THE GREAT FUCKING BEYOND.
I NEED YOU TO DELIVER WHAT YOU PROMISED ME. MONEY.
DON'T WORRY. YOU'LL GET YOUR MONEY. AND WHETHER YOU LIKE IT OR NOT, YOU'RE GONNA BE PART OF CHANGING THE WORLD AND MAKING IT A SLIGHTLY BETTER PLACE.
IT WILL BE A MUCH BETTER WORLD ONCE I'M A BILLIONAIRE, I AGREE.

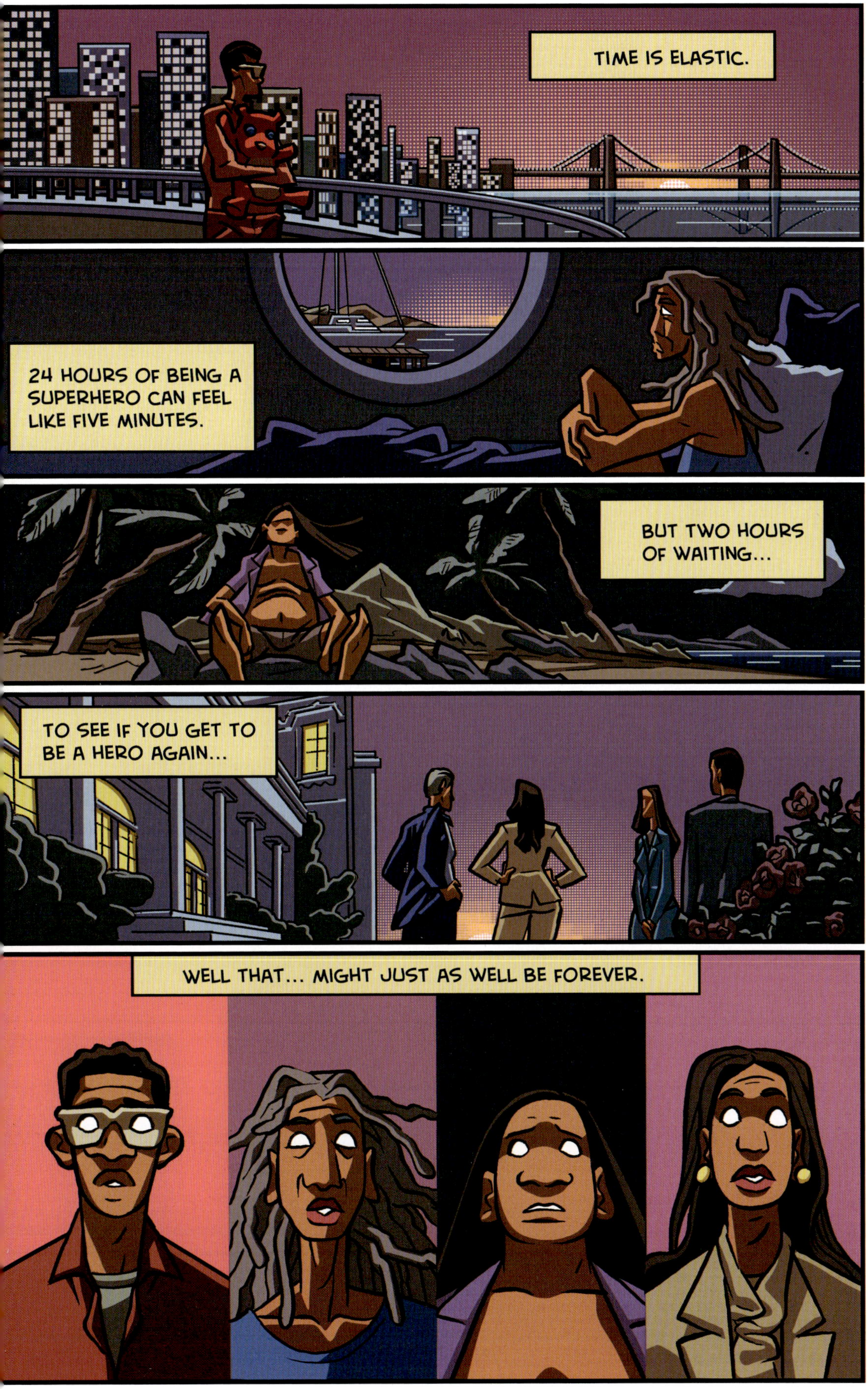
TIME IS ELASTIC.
24 HOURS OF BEING A SUPERHERO CAN FEEL LIKE FIVE MINUTES.
BUT TWO HOURS OF WAITING...
TO SEE IF YOU GET TO BE A HERO AGAIN...
WELL THAT... MIGHT JUST AS WELL BE FOREVER.

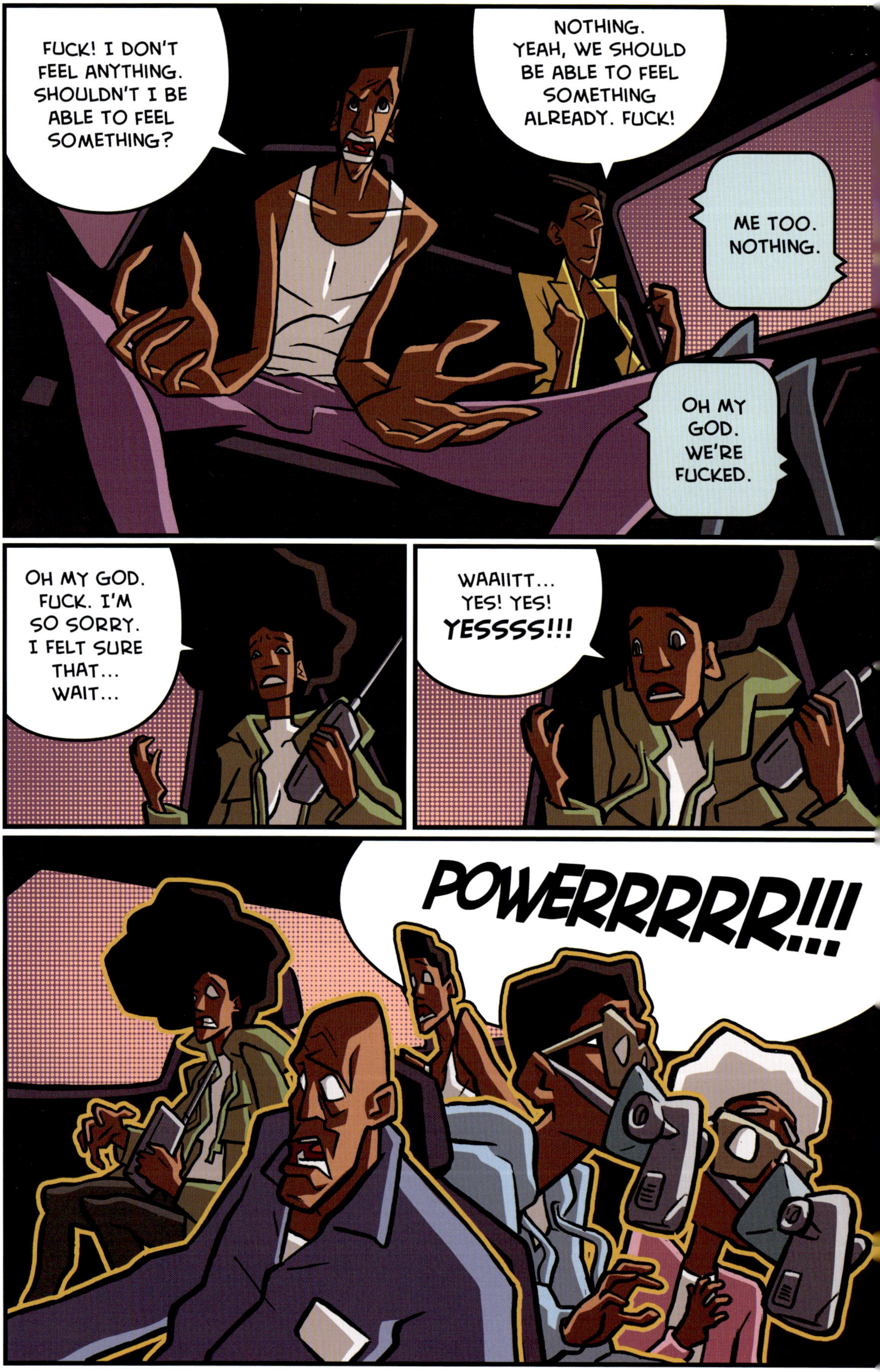
FUCK! I DON'T FEEL ANYTHING. SHOULDN'T I BE ABLE TO FEEL SOMETHING?
NOTHING. YEAH, WE SHOULD BE ABLE TO FEEL SOMETHING ALREADY. FUCK!
ME TOO. NOTHING.
OH MY GOD. WE'RE FUCKED.
OH MY GOD. FUCK. I'M SO SORRY. I FELT SURE THAT... WAIT...
WAAIITT... YES! YES! YESSSS!!!
POWERRRRRR!!!

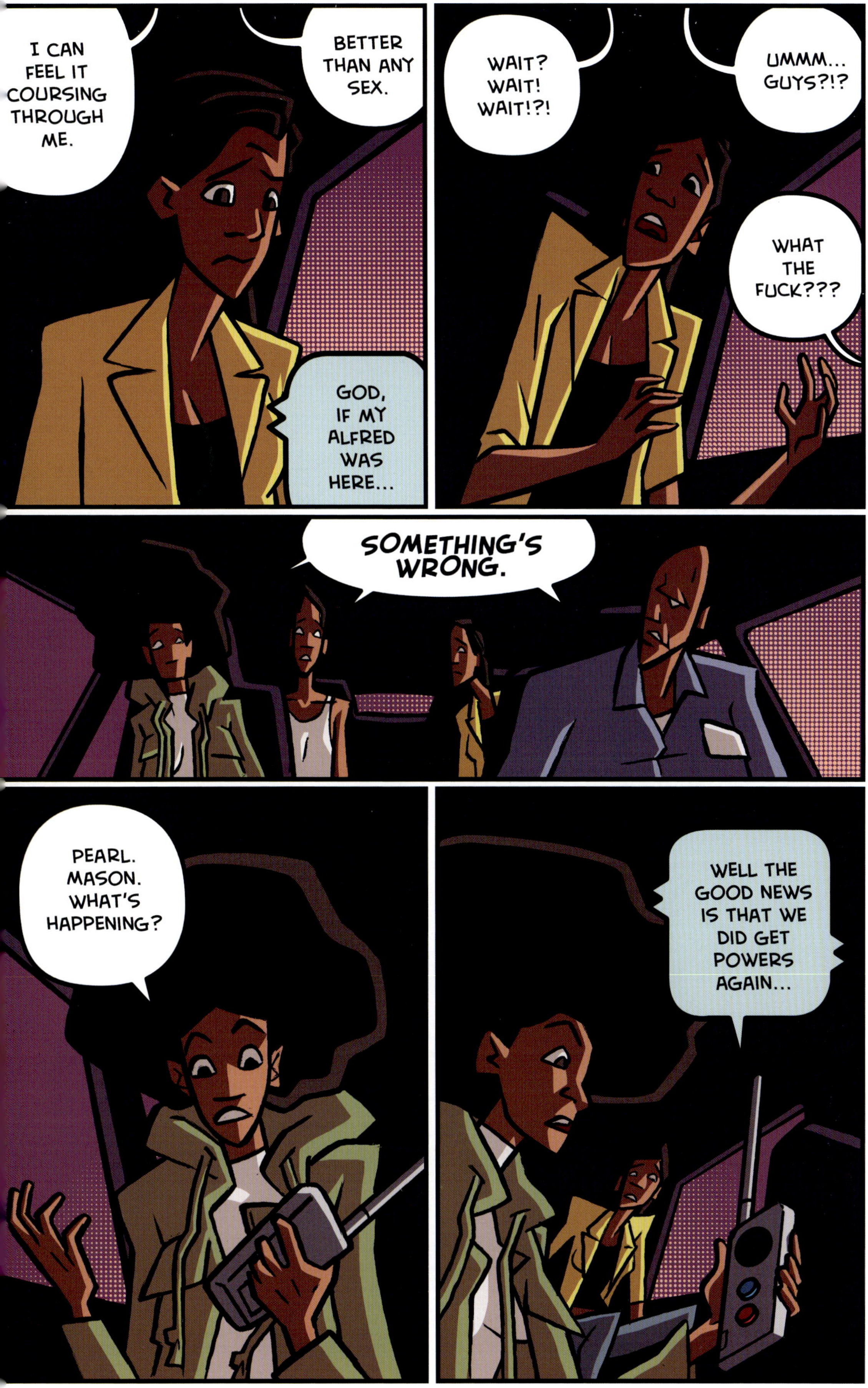
I CAN FEEL IT COURSING THROUGH ME.
BETTER THAN ANY SEX.
GOD, IF MY ALFRED WAS HERE...
WAIT? WAIT! WAIT!?!
UMMM... GUYS?!?
WHAT THE FUCK???
SOMETHING'S WRONG.
PEARL. MASON. WHAT'S HAPPENING?
WELL THE GOOD NEWS IS THAT WE DID GET POWERS AGAIN...

THE BAD NEWS IS... THEY APPEAR TO BE DIFFERENT.
WRITTEN BY TRAVON FREE & MARTIN DESMOND ROE
ART BY AREMO MASSA

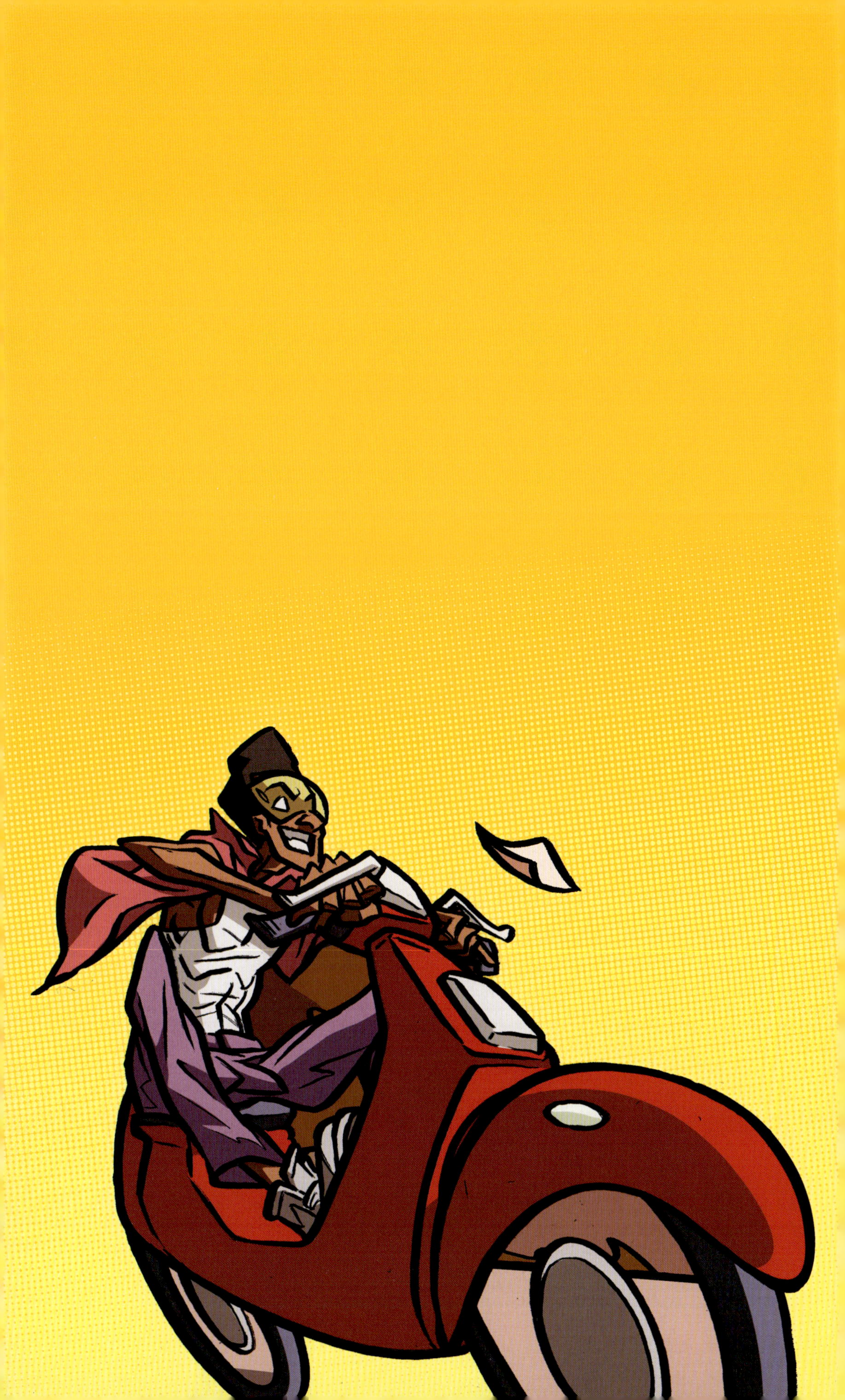

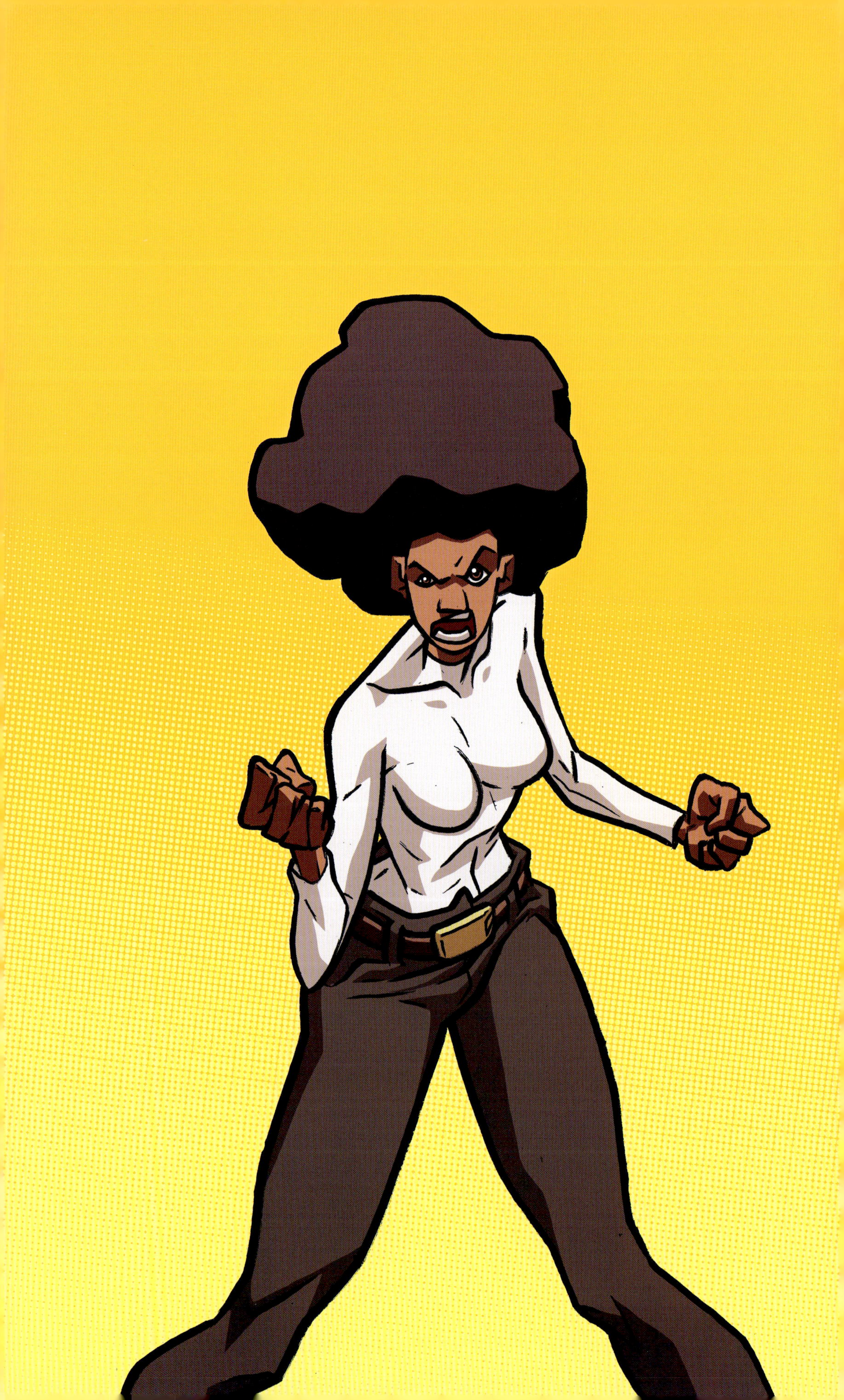

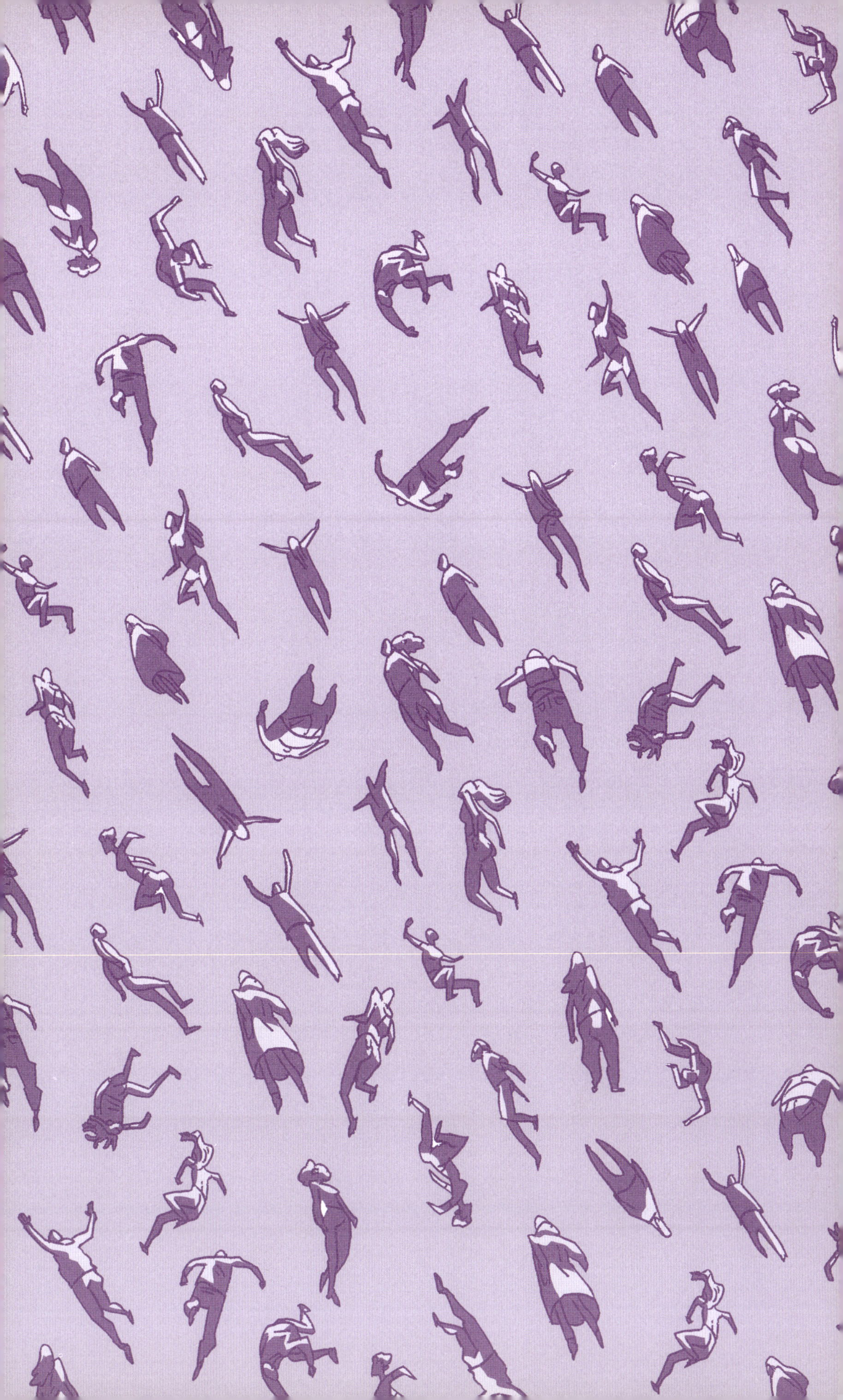

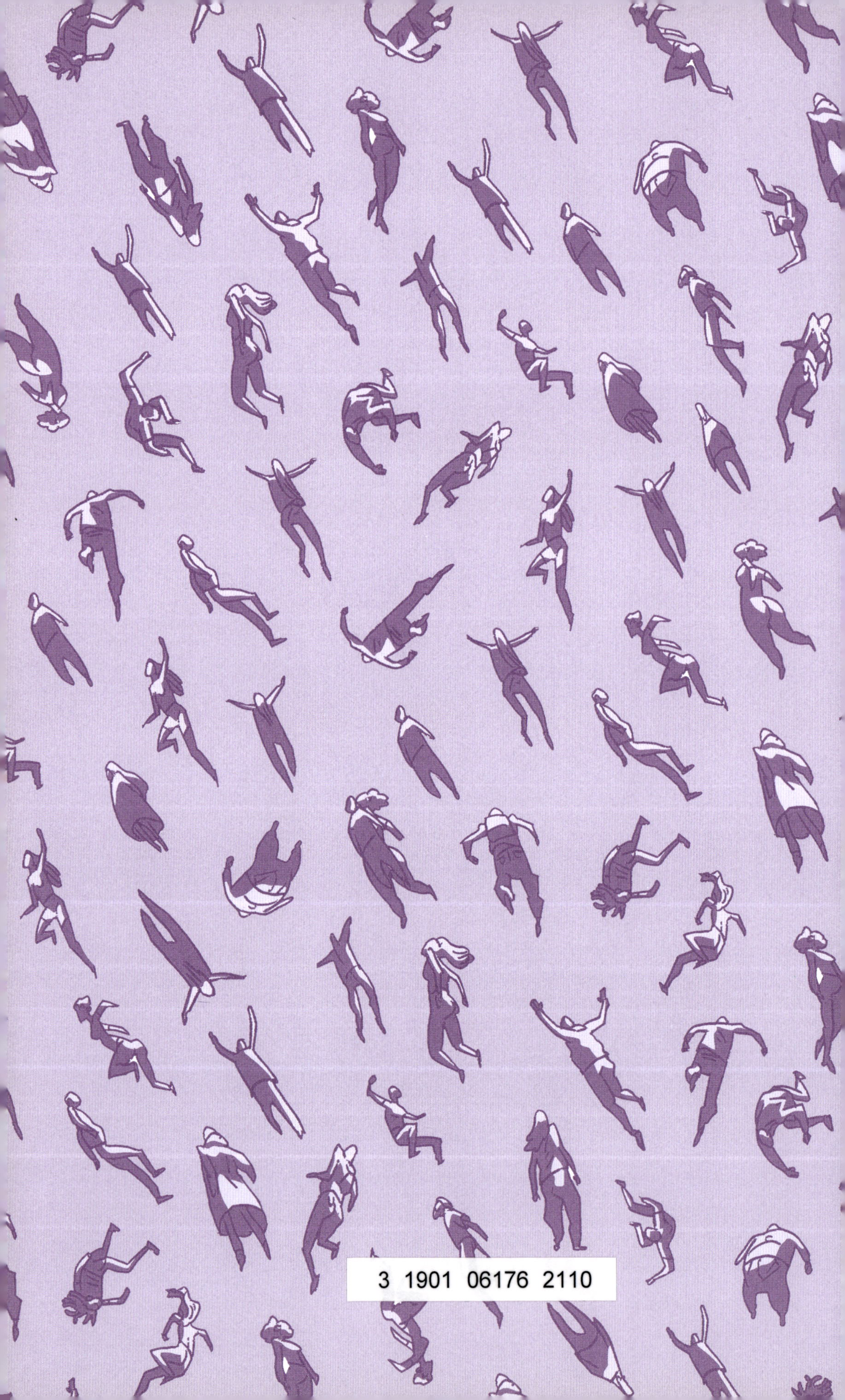